I couldn't believe my eyes. Samara was standing on a stool, wearing her red dress, while Heavenly did final alterations. Only Samara wasn't actually touching the stool. She was *floating* about four inches above it!

I quickly looked around to see if anyone else had noticed.

Wes was packing up the sewing machine. Tyler was sitting in his high chair eating cut-up pieces of banana. Robby's face was buried in a *Mad* magazine. The puppy was on the floor, licking his paw.

No one appeared to be aware that Samara was floating. Not even Samara!

"Ahem!" I cleared my throat loudly.

Thump! Samara landed on the stool and looked startled.

"Finished?" I asked Heavenly.

"Yes," she answered.

From Archway Paperbacks

Here Comes Heavenly #1
Here Comes Heavenly #2: Dance Magic

Published by Pocket Books

From Minstrel Books

AGAINST THE ODDS™: Shark Bite
AGAINST THE ODDS™: Grizzly Attack
AGAINST THE ODDS™: Buzzard's Feast
AGAINST THE ODDS™: Gator Prey

Published by Pocket Books

HERE COMES HEAVENLY

DANCE MAGIC

Todd Strasser

AN ARCHWAY PAPERBACK
Published by POCKET BOOKS
New York   London   Toronto   Sydney   Singapore

AN ARCHWAY PAPERBACK *Original*

 An Archway Paperback published by
POCKET BOOKS, a division of Simon & Schuster Inc.
1230 Avenue of the Americas, New York, NY 10020

Copyright © 1999 by Todd Strasser

ISBN: 0-671-03627-0

First Archway Paperback printing December 1999

10   9   8   7   6   5   4   3   2

AN ARCHWAY PAPERBACK and colophon are registered trademarks of Simon & Schuster Inc.

Front cover illustration by Miro Sinovcic

Printed in the U.S.A.

IL 5+

for Sophie, Nina,
and Meghan Ryan

Chapter

"**M**arwich rots! Marwich rots!**"** the crowd of kids from Soundview Manor chanted. We were sitting in the stands at Marwich High School, rooting for our team, the Soundview Sonics, against our arch rivals, the Marwich Marauders.

"*Soundview stinks! Soundview stinks!*" From across the soccer field came the reply from the Marwich fans, waving their black-and-orange school banners. The fans from both schools had been shouting at each other for nearly half an hour. Meanwhile, the score in the game was tied 1–1.

I was sitting in the stands with various friends and members of my family, including Heavenly Litebody, the new nanny.

"The fans certainly are rabid," Heavenly said. She was sitting in the row behind me, bouncing two-year-old Tyler on her knee. It was a crisp clear fall day, and Heavenly was wearing her baggy brown sweater and bright red scarf. Tyler, dressed in blue corduroy pants, a teal jacket, and a red knit cap, was busy gnawing on a hard pretzel.

"We really hate Marwich," I explained as I waved a blue-and-white Soundview High banner. Marwich was the town next to Soundview Manor, and the rivalry between the two schools had been going on forever.

"We don't just hate them, we despise them," added my best friend, Darcy Schultz, who was sitting on my left. Darcy's long black hair was braided into pigtails. She'd worn a blue-and-white scarf to the game, and now she took it off her neck and waved it in the air.

Sitting on my right was Roy Chandler, the boy I'd had a crush on for years. Roy had painted his face half white and half blue, the Soundview colors. He'd brought a bugle to the game, and now he jumped to his feet and turned to face the crowd. After blowing some loud, trilling notes on the bugle, he made a fist and led a chant:

"Two, four, six, eight, who will we annihilate?
Marwich! Marwich! Mar . . . wich rots!"

Then he sat back down, breathing hard. "We can't let those jerks from Marwich win. We really can't!"

Down on the field, the black-and-white soccer ball bounced back and forth between the players on the two teams. One of the players most responsible for not letting Marwich win was my stepbrother, Chance, who played the sweeper position for Soundview.

The sweeper was the last line of defense before the goalie, and Chance played it with a passion. His shin guards and legs were covered with grass stains and streaks of dirt. His light brown hair hung in sweaty spikes down his forehead. As both teams fought for the ball, he prowled the area in front of the goalie like a wild animal intent on defending his home.

Just then a gasp went through the Soundview fans as three players from the Marwich team dribbled the ball deep into Soundview territory. Loud cheers and screams came from the Marwich stands as their side smelled a score coming.

"It's three on one!" Roy cried in horror.

"Oh, Chance!" Heavenly cheered. "Don't let them score!"

Down on the field, the three Marwich players closed in on the goal. Chance crouched down, watching and waiting to spring. We knew that if he charged the player with the ball, that player could pass to one of his teammates and have an open kick on the goal.

It all depended on Chance. . . .

Suddenly he leaned to his right.

The Marwich player with the ball saw him move and instantly passed the ball to the player on Chance's left.

But out of nowhere, Chance was there! He dived toward the ball and smacked it with his head, sending it back up the field, where another Soundview player took over.

A huge groan came from the Marwich stands. At the same time a cheer rose out of the Soundview stands.

"He did it!" Roy shouted gleefully. "Did you see that? He faked him out! He made him think he was going right, then he went left and broke up the play!"

"That was fantastic!" Heavenly cried.

I beamed with pride, knowing that for the moment my stepbrother was the hero.

The referee blew his whistle twice. It was halftime. The Marwich players trudged toward their side of the field with their heads hanging in disappointment. The Soundview players crowded around Chance, rubbing his head gratefully and patting him on the back. They all had huge smiles on their faces as they trotted toward our side of the field. Even the high school soccer coach came out onto the field to congratulate Chance and shake his hand.

"Did anyone ever tell you your stepbrother was amazing?" Darcy asked me.

"About a thousand times," I said.

Behind us a bunch of older girls stood up. All at once they shouted, "We love you, Chance!"

Down on the field, Chance brushed the sweaty hair out of his eyes and looked up at them. He smiled and waved. The girls started to giggle.

Darcy looked back at them and then at me. "Isn't Chance in tenth grade?" she asked in a low voice.

"Yes," I answered.

"Well, two of those girls who just yelled they loved him are juniors," Darcy whispered. "And the third one's a senior!"

"Doesn't matter how old they are," I whispered back. "They all love him."

"Hey, everyone loves a winner," Roy pointed out.

"Just don't forget, it's only the first half," I said. "We still haven't won."

"Maybe not," said Roy, "but you better believe that those Marwich guys are really depressed right now. They're probably wondering what magic spell they'll have to conjure up to beat us."

I looked back at Heavenly and asked, "Know any good magic soccer spells?"

Heavenly just smiled back at me and didn't say a word. I guess I should explain about Heavenly and what she was doing in my family. We had what you'd call a blended family. Chance and his sister, Samara, were Dad's kids. My brother Robby and I were Mom's kids. Tyler belonged to both of them. Mom and Dad were always away on business trips, and Heavenly was the most recent of Tyler's many nannies. About a month before, Heavenly had "magically" appeared in our kitchen, insisting she was the new nanny. Since then some pretty strange things had happened—things that made me seriously wonder if she did indeed know some magic spells.

Since it was half-time, people were getting up to stretch their legs and leave the stands to get refreshments. But my friends and I remained seated.

"Bug," said Tyler, who was still sitting on Heavenly's lap. A red ladybug was crawling on his finger. Tyler stared at it with intense fascination.

That was another strange thing about Heavenly. Ever since she'd arrived, there were always ladybugs around—even now in the late fall when it was cold and almost every other kind of insect had disappeared.

Tyler slowly picked up the ladybug between his little thumb and forefinger and began to squeeze it.

Heavenly had been gazing off at the crowd when she suddenly winced and looked down at Tyler.

"No!" she cried, and quickly grabbed my little brother's hand before he could crush the ladybug. "Never, ever, hurt a living creature! Especially a ladybug!"

Tyler gave her a wide-eyed startled look. Darcy and I shared a puzzled glance.

"Why?" Tyler asked innocently.

"Because," replied Heavenly, who seemed surprisingly rattled by the whole thing. I mean, after all, it was only a bug.

"My mom said you should never accept 'because' as a reason," Darcy said.

Heavenly blinked at us and for a moment didn't seem to know what to say. Then she said, "Has anyone seen Samara and the puppy?"

Darcy, Roy and I looked around. Heavenly was right. Samara, my twelve-year-old stepsister, had disappeared.

Chapter

It was strange that Samara had disappeared. Then again, it was strange that she'd come to the game in the first place. We'd all been totally surprised that morning when Samara announced that she was going. Samara usually couldn't care less about sports.

I was even more suspicious when she got dressed up and insisted on bringing our new puppy to the game. I couldn't imagine her sitting in the stands the whole time with the puppy in her lap.

But we'd gotten to the field and I'd immediately become distracted by the game.

"Now that I think of it," I said, "I'm not sure I ever saw her in the stands."

"I thought she said something about taking the dog for a walk," Darcy said.

"You'd better go look for her," Heavenly advised.

"Sure." Roy started to stand. "I feel like stretching my legs anyway. Let's see if we can find her."

Darcy, Roy, and I climbed down out of the stands and started to walk along the side of the soccer field.

"Do you know what Heavenly just did?" Darcy asked in a low voice so Roy wouldn't hear.

"She told us to look for Samara," I said.

"*Before* that," Darcy said.

"Uh, she stopped Tyler from squashing the ladybug."

"No, *after* that," said Darcy.

"What?" I asked.

"She changed the subject," Darcy said. "We asked her why she got so freaked over the ladybug, and instead of answering, she asked us to go find Samara."

"You're right!" I realized.

"There's something about her," Darcy said. "I just can't quite figure out what it is."

I knew she was right. There were lots of things about Heavenly I couldn't quite figure out, either. Like why she wore her dyed purple hair short and spiky. And why her eyebrow and nose were pierced. Where she'd come from and how she'd gotten past the security system that guarded our house. Sometimes I'd get really curious about it, but other times I'd decide it simply didn't matter.

But Darcy was the kind of person who loved a

mystery. She was always reading mystery stories and doing jigsaw puzzles.

"Hey!" Roy suddenly stopped and pointed across the field at the Marwich stands. "Isn't that her?"

We peered across the field. Samara was standing on the Marwich side, near the stands where the Marwich fans were sitting. She was holding the red leash of our new puppy, a golden retriever, but she seemed to be looking up at the stands.

"Roy, can I use your binoculars?" I asked.

"Sure." Roy pulled the binocular strap over his head and handed them to me. He had come to the game with not only a bugle and binoculars but with a hat and sunscreen as well. I guess you could say that Roy was a born Boy Scout.

I pressed the binoculars to my eyes and took a closer look at my stepsister. She was looking up into the Marwich stands at a group of boys about her age. The boys were leaning against the rail. At their center was a boy who was taller than the others. While I was too far away to tell for sure, he appeared to be very, very good-looking.

"I don't believe it," I said, handing the binoculars back to Roy.

"What?" asked Darcy.

"Guess why she's over on the Marwich side of the field?" I said.

"Spying?" Roy guessed.

"Right, but not on the other team," I said. "She's spying on a boy."

"A boy?" Roy repeated. "Samara?"

"I didn't think she was interested in boys," said Darcy.

"Neither did I," I said. "I always thought the only person she was interested in was herself."

"Not nice, Kit," Darcy said in a mildly scolding tone.

"I know," I admitted. "But it's true."

"Hey, wait a minute!" Roy was peering across the field with the binoculars. "Now what's she doing?"

I quickly took the binoculars from him and pressed them to my eyes. Samara had let go of the puppy's leash!

Not only that, but she seemed to be shooing the puppy under the Marwich stands!

Chapter

3

I don't believe her!" I grumbled.

"Now what?" Darcy asked.

"She just let go of the puppy," I said.

"Why?" asked Roy.

With my bare eyes I could see what Samara did next. She called up to the boys in the stands, then pointed under the stands where our puppy was sniffing around.

"She is just unbelievable!" I fumed. "It's the old damsel-with-a-puppy–in–distress act! She let go of the puppy, and now she wants those boys to help her find him. Come on, let's go!"

"Where?" Darcy asked.

"To get the puppy," I said. "I don't care if Samara wants to go fishing for boys, but I'll be darned if I'll let her use our puppy as bait."

"Right!" Roy cried. "That's puppy abuse!"

Roy tooted the bugle and then hurried with Darcy and me around the field. By now the group of Marwich boys had crawled under the stands and was chasing the puppy around the metal supports.

Samara, of course, didn't join the chase. She was too busy talking to the tall, good-looking boy I'd spotted in the stands.

"If anything happens to that puppy, I'll kill her!" I muttered as I ran. I admit I was just being dramatic. The puppy probably thought it was a lot of fun to be chased around.

A moment later I reached my stepsister. She was still talking to the boy, who, I could now see, was absolutely striking. He appeared to be Samara's age, but he was taller than most twelve-year-olds, and he had the most amazing blue eyes I'd ever seen. He also had a deep tan, which was kind of unusual for the late fall. Talking to Samara, he seemed very relaxed and self-assured.

"Uh, excuse me!" I muttered as I joined them.

Samara spun around and frowned when she saw me. "What are you doing here, Kit?"

"I'm looking for our puppy," I said. "It seems that you let him go."

"Who's this?" the good-looking boy asked.

"Oh, it's just my sister, Kit," Samara said. "My *stepsister*, that is. Kit, this is Parker Marks. Maybe you've seen him in the Asphalt Clothes catalog or on TV in the Blast Cola commercial."

"You're a model?" Darcy asked, instantly star-struck.

"Well, yeah." Parker Marks shrugged as if it was no big deal.

"I've never met a male model before." Darcy was practically drooling.

"Well, now you have." Samara stepped between them as if to make sure Darcy didn't get any closer.

"Why did you let the puppy go?" I asked.

"I didn't *let* the puppy go," Samara corrected me. "He got away."

"Oh, give me a—" I was just about to put her in her place when one of the Marwich boys came out from under the stands with our puppy in his arms.

"Look what I found!" he said with a grin.

"My puppy!" Samara cried as if she'd been incredibly worried about him. She scooped the puppy into her arms and squeezed him. Our puppy yipped happily and licked Samara on the chin.

"Naughty puppy!" she pretended to scold him. "Don't you ever run away from Samara again!"

"Talk about acting!" I grumbled in total disgust. What a phony my stepsister was! What a fake!

Meanwhile, Parker Marks's friends were giving Roy funny looks.

"Hey," said one of them, "aren't you a Soundview fan?"

"I am?" Roy answered nervously. I guess he'd forgotten that he'd painted his face blue and white.

"Yeah, you're the bugle guy," said another. He turned to Darcy and me. "You're all wearing blue and white. You guys must be crazy to be on this side of the field."

"Crazy," Roy sputtered in fear as he started to back away. "That's exactly right! We are crazy! Completely wacko!"

I felt Darcy tug at my sleeve. "Come on, Kit, I think it's time for us to go back to the other side of the field."

"Oh, Kit, think you could do me a favor and take the puppy with you?" Samara handed the puppy's leash to me and turned back to Parker Marks. She wasn't wearing any blue or white, so I guess nobody cared which side she was rooting for.

"I can't believe what a phony she is!" I mumbled as the three of us walked quickly toward our side of the field. "I mean, letting go of the puppy and then pretending it had gotten away by accident. How low can you go?"

"Did you see that boy?" Darcy asked dreamily.

"So he's a model," I said. "Big deal."

"It is a big deal," Darcy said. "Have you ever met a model before?"

"He's twelve, Darcy. That's two years younger than you."

"That doesn't mean I can't drool over him," Darcy said.

"Oh, gross!" Roy wrinkled his blue-and-white nose. "Drool over him? Can't you find a better way to describe it?"

"Spare me," I groaned.

"Oh, come on, Kit," Darcy said. "Don't tell me you're jealous just because your sister's discovered a gorgeous boy."

Roy instantly gave me a worried look. "You're not jealous, are you, Kit?"

"Believe me, I couldn't be farther from jealousy," I assured him. "I'm more grossed out than anything. You have to understand my stepsister. What Samara wants, Samara gets. Nothing stops her. I mean, absolutely nothing. Up until now, that mostly meant clothes. But if it's going to start including boys, heaven help us *and* them."

Chapter

We got back to the Soundview stands just as everyone took their seats for the second half. My friends and I climbed back to our seats. The puppy must have been tired, because he went to sleep in my lap.

The second half began. I really couldn't believe Samara. She spent almost the entire time with her back to the game, talking to Parker Marks.

"Uh, Kit?" Darcy said at one point.

"What?" I asked.

"Enjoying the game?"

"What? No—I mean, yes."

"That's funny," Darcy said, "because you've spent the whole time watching Samara."

"I just can't get over her," I fumed. "Do you know she hasn't looked at the game once?"

"Neither have you," Darcy pointed out.

"That's different," I insisted. "I'm not using this game just as an excuse to spend time with some boy."

"Too bad," Roy said with a sigh.

"I'm serious!" I said.

"I know." Roy nodded, a little sadly.

"Maybe you ought to forget about Samara for now," Heavenly suggested.

Just then a loud cheer rose out of the stands as Soundview scored its second goal. We were winning 2–1!

For the rest of the game I actually did manage to watch. Soundview kept the lead despite everything Marwich threw at them. With about a minute to go, the Marwich players broke free and drove the ball close to the Soundview goal.

Once again Chance was there to meet them. Sensing this was their last chance to score, the Marwich fans were on their feet cheering. Everyone on the Soundview side rose to their feet, too, but we were silent, praying Chance would come through.

"Three on one, again," Roy muttered.

"Only this time they know what to expect," Heavenly added.

The three Marwich players closed in on the goal. Chance crouched and waited. You could almost see the Marwich forwards planning their move.

Suddenly Chance leaned to his right.

The Marwich player with the ball saw him, only this time, instead of passing the ball to the player on Chance's left, he passed it to the player on his right.

And once again Chance seemed to come out of nowhere! He slid to the ball and sent it rolling out of bounds!

A huge cheer rose out of the Soundview stands.

"He did it!" Roy shouted gleefully. "Did you see that? He reverse-faked him! He made him think he was going right, and then he actually did go right!"

Suddenly loud murmurs and shouts erupted around us. Down on the field, one of the Marwich players was wrestling Chance to the ground!

"Boo!" "Bad sport!" "Throw him out!" All around us Soundview fans shouted angrily at the Marwich player who'd started the scuffle.

The referee ran toward them, blowing his whistle. The coaches and players from both teams ran out onto the field.

"It's a soccer riot!" Roy shouted. "Oh, wow! I thought they only did this in Europe!"

But there was no riot. The players simply pulled Chance and the other boy apart. Then the referee gave them both red cards.

"What's that?" Darcy asked.

"Dinner invitations," Roy said.

"Really?"

"No, they're red cards," I explained. "It means they both get thrown out of the game."

"But that's not fair," Heavenly complained. "Chance didn't do anything. The other boy started it."

"Everyone knows that," Roy said, "but with the way both sides are feeling right now, if the ref only threw the Marwich player out of the game, there *really* would be a riot."

"But without Chance, Marwich might score and tie it up," Darcy said.

"I figure the ref knows there isn't enough time," Roy speculated, checking his watch.

He was right; play had hardly started again when the referee blew the whistle three times, ending the game.

"We won!" Roy shouted, thrusting a triumphant fist into the air and blowing his bugle.

The Soundview Manor crowd started to climb down from the stands. Since we were Chance's family, we went down to the field to congratulate him. When we got there, everyone was standing around Chance and Coach Flemming. As usual, Chance's uniform was dirtier and grimier than that of every other player on the team.

"Chance, you saved the game for us twice today," Coach Flemming was saying. "You know I like to stress that it's a team effort and no one can win a game by himself, but just this once I think your teammates would agree that you were definitely today's MVP."

"Darn right!" said Chance's friend Jared, who played forward for the Sonics. The rest of Chance's teammates clapped.

"So that's it, boys," Coach Flemming said. "I'll see you all at practice tomorrow."

The team began to drift away, but not before a few more fans came up and congratulated Chance on his playing. Finally it was just us and him. Chance had a sheepish expression on his face and looked a little red. But it wasn't from the exercise. He was embarrassed by all the attention.

"You're a hero, Chance," Heavenly said.

"Not really. If you want to know the truth, it was mostly luck," Chance said.

"You're just saying that," said Heavenly.

"No, I'm not," Chance insisted. "The first time they came down field, I faked right and went left. If the guy on the other team had gone right, they probably would have scored. The second time I faked right and went right, but it was just luck. Anytime it's three on one, you need a lot of luck."

"Whatever it was, we're proud of you," I said.

Chance smiled a little. "Thanks, Kit, I appreciate that."

Thick gray clouds had begun to drift overhead, blocking out the last afternoon sun. It felt cold in the clouds' shadows. In Heavenly's arms Tyler started to whimper.

"He's cold and tired," Heavenly said. "I probably should have taken him home already, but the game was too exciting. We'd better head back now."

"Wait a minute," I said. "Where's Samara?"

We all looked over at the Marwich side of the field. Only a few Marwich fans were still around, and most of them were leaving.

Samara was nowhere in sight.

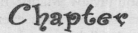

Where could she be?" Heavenly asked.

"The last time we saw her, she was talking to Parker Marks," I said.

"Who?" Chance asked.

We explained that Parker Marks was a kid who went to Marwich Middle School and also happened to be an actor and model.

"Figures," Chance said with a smirk.

"What do you mean?" I asked.

"You wouldn't expect Samara to be interested in anyone *average*, would you?" he asked.

"We can't just go home and leave her," Heavenly said.

"Then we'd better go find her," Chance said.

"Not you." I held up my hand.

Chance stopped. "Why not?"

"Because we're in Marwich, Chance," I said.

"They hate Soundview Manor here, and right now they hate us more than ever. That guy attacked you on the field even though there were coaches and refs around. Think of what will happen if anyone sees you walking around town in a Soundview Sonics uniform."

"I don't care," Chance said and tried to step past me.

"Maybe you don't, but I do," I said, blocking his path.

Chance stopped and looked at me. I stared right back at him. As usual, his piercing gaze made me shiver, but I was serious. "You can't walk around Marwich in that uniform, Chance. You'll get hurt."

To my relief, Chance nodded. "Okay, I'll go home and shower and change, but you'd better call when you find her. If you haven't called by the time I get out of the shower, I'm coming back here."

"It's a deal," I said, handing the puppy's leash to Heavenly.

"Wait, I'm coming with you," said Darcy, unwrapping the blue-and-white scarf from around her neck.

"Me, too," said Roy.

"With your face painted white and blue?" I asked. "I don't think so."

Roy rubbed his hand against his face and stared at the white-and-blue makeup that came off on his fingers. "All right, I'll go home and wash this stuff off, but it's the same deal. If you don't call, I'm coming back to find you."

"Fair enough," I said.

"Be careful," Heavenly said. "If you find yourselves in any trouble, I want you to call right away."

"Gotcha," I said.

Darcy and I started down the sidewalk toward the town of Marwich.

"That was cute of Chance and Roy," Darcy said.

"You mean, wanting to come with us?" I asked.

"It was like they wanted to protect us," she said.

"I can see Chance protecting us, but it's hard to imagine Roy that way," I said. Roy was slight and thin and about three inches shorter than me.

"That's what was so cute," Darcy said. "He's so totally in Crushland over you."

"I know," I said. "It's so strange. Hardly a night goes by that he doesn't call twice, and he always wants to do things with me after school and on the weekends. It might actually be annoying if he wasn't so sweet."

"Isn't it weird?" Darcy asked. "I mean, I know he always liked you as a friend. But it used to be *you* who had the crush on *him*. How did it get turned around?"

"I'm not sure, but I have a funny feeling Heavenly had something to do with it," I said.

"How?" Darcy asked.

"Promise you'll keep it a secret and not tell a soul?" I asked.

"Promise," Darcy said.

I reminded her of how Jessica "Have It All" Huffington had snaked Roy from me as a partner in the history project at school a few weeks before. And how, after I'd told Heavenly about it, Jessica suddenly invited me to join them as a third partner and Roy had started acting like he was insanely in love with me.

"You really think she had something to do with it?" Darcy asked.

"I'm not sure," I said. "I mean, what could she have done? Put a spell on them? It sounds crazy. But I can't think of any other way to explain it."

"That reminds me of something I found out and forgot to tell you about," Darcy said. Her mother was the president of the Soundview Manor Historical Society, and her father was a college history professor. They were the kind of family who enjoyed nothing more than sifting through dusty old history books.

"Remember I told you that the Litebodys were the original settlers of Soundview Manor and that they all mysteriously disappeared around the time of the Great Depression?" Darcy said. "Well, here's something else. You know the Shackelford Semiconductor Company?"

"Of course I do, Darcy. How could you live

in Soundview Manor and *not* know about them?"

"Well, the other day I was in the library looking at some old photographs, and I found one of a big brick building that's no longer around. Guess what it said on the front of the building?"

"Just tell me, Darcy," I said.

"Shackelford and Litebody," Darcy said.

I stopped and looked at her. "Really?"

"Yup." Darcy nodded.

"What kind of building was it?"

"It looked like some kind of factory, but I couldn't really tell," Darcy said. "But isn't it interesting? The Shackelfords go on to become the richest and most powerful family in Soundview Manor while the Litebodys disappear."

"That's *very* interesting," I said as we started to walk again. "Let me ask you something, Darcy. Think you could find that photograph and make a copy of it?"

"Sure."

We were entering the village of Marwich now. There were a lot of people on the sidewalks, including some kids wearing the orange-and-black Marwich colors.

"Think we'll be okay?" Darcy asked nervously.

"Sure," I said. "We're just a couple of kids walking around. Why should anyone suspect we're from Soundview?"

"Know what's strange?" Darcy asked as we

passed a Starbucks coffeeshop and a bank. "I never come here. I mean, it's the town next to ours, but for the number of times I've been here, it could be a million miles away."

"I know," I said. "It's like we either hang around in our own town or go to the mall. Why bother to go anywhere else?"

A couple of older girls came toward us on the sidewalk wearing orange-and-black Marwich High sweaters. I could feel Darcy tense beside me.

"Don't worry," I whispered, "they can't tell where we're from."

The girls passed and Darcy breathed easier. "I know it doesn't make sense," she said. "But it just feels weird to be here right now. Like if they knew we were from Soundview, we'd be burned at the stake."

We turned the corner, still looking for Samara. We peeked in the window of a pizza place, then in the ultra-fancy dress store next to it.

"Wow, can you believe the prices on these dresses?" Darcy gasped as we looked in the window.

"Outrageous," I said. "They must be from some famous designer."

"They even have young miss and little kids' sizes," Darcy pointed out.

"Yeah, but the only people who could afford dresses like these are old rich ladies," I said.

Darcy and I chuckled. Suddenly I heard voices. A pack of boys was coming down the sidewalk toward us. They were carrying black-and-orange banners and looked about Samara's age. As they got closer, I realized they were the same bunch of boys who'd chased us away from the Marwich side of the field during the game.

I turned to the dress store window. "Whatever you do, don't look," I whispered to Darcy.

"Why not?" she whispered back.

"Because these guys might actually recognize us."

The boys were coming closer. Darcy and I pretended to stare into the dress store window. I held my breath. I don't know why I should have been nervous. As long as they didn't get a good look at our faces, there was no reason for them to suspect anything.

The boys passed behind us. I started to breath easier. And that's when I blew it.

I turned to watch them go, and just as I did, one of them looked back.

Suddenly he stopped and frowned.

Uh-oh! I quickly nudged Darcy with my elbow. "Don't look now," I whispered, "but I think we just got nailed."

Meanwhile, the boy stopped his friends and said something in a low voice I couldn't hear.

Now they were all staring at us.

"What do we do?" Darcy whispered.

"Find someplace to hide," I whispered back.

The boys started back toward us. It's true that

they were two years younger than we were, but there were five of them and only two of us.

"Hide where?" Darcy asked.

Good question, I thought.

"Hey, you two!" one of the boys yelled.

I grabbed Darcy by the wrist and pulled her into the dress store.

Chapter 6

Darcy and I headed for the back of the store where the changing rooms were. The Marwich boys milled around on the sidewalk outside, giving us threatening looks and gestures, but not daring to come in.

"Brilliant, Kit," Darcy said with a sigh of relief. "There's no way one of those boys would dare come into a store like this."

"Let's just hope they get bored and leave," I said.

"I think they will," said Darcy. "I don't think they can stand even hanging around *outside* a dress store for long."

I grinned. "Hope you're right."

Feeling confident that we were safe in the dress store, we started to look around.

"You have to admit, some of this stuff is really

31

beautiful," Darcy said as she thumbed through a rack of dresses.

I pulled a slinky little black number off the rack and held it up. It was hardly bigger than a dish towel and the fabric was as thin as tissue. "Oh, my gosh!"

"What?" Darcy asked.

"Look at the price tag."

Darcy nodded. "It proves my theory about dresses. The less there is, the more they cost."

Suddenly the sound of off-key singing came from one of the dressing rooms. It was that song from the show *West Side Story:*

I feel pretty, oh so pretty . . .

Darcy grimaced and whispered. "Wow, I don't know who that is, but she really can't carry a tune!"

Meanwhile, I felt the blood drain out of my face.

"What's with you?" Darcy asked.

"I think I know who that is!" I groaned.

Just at that moment the dressing room door flew open and Samara pranced out, humming to herself. She was wearing the slinkiest little low-cut red dress with bikini straps and a slit.

She stopped humming when she saw us. "What are you doing here?"

"Looking for you," I said, staring at the dress.

"How'd you know I was here?" my stepsister asked.

"We didn't," I said. "We were chased in here by a bunch of bloodthirsty Marwich boys. Friends, I might add, of Parker Marks."

"Was he with them?" Samara asked eagerly.

"No."

Samara's shoulders sagged with disappointment.

"Samara," I said, "what in the world are you doing in here?"

Samara brightened. "Isn't this place fabulous? I mean, here we are, just one town over from Soundview Manor. Who could have imagined that a place like this existed in Marwich?"

"You still haven't answered my question," I said. "What are *you* doing here?"

"Trying stuff on, of course," Samara said, then twirled around on her toes, showing off the red dress. "Do you like it?"

"It doesn't matter whether I like it," I said. "Girls your age don't wear dresses like that. Girls your age can't *afford* dresses like that."

Samara stuck her nose in the air. "I could get Mom to buy this for me if I wanted."

"How?" I asked.

"Easy," Samara said. "All I'd have to do is lay on the guilt trip. You know, about how hard it is to grow up with a mother who's away almost all the time. That *always* gets her."

"But what's the point?" Darcy asked. "Even if she got you that dress, you'd never wear it."

"Yes, I would," Samara insisted.

"When?" I asked.

"When the right opportunity came along," Samara said.

"Well, I don't know when that'll be," I said. "But right now we have the opportunity to go home, and that's exactly what we're going to do."

Samara, of course, saw no reason why she couldn't stay and try on more dresses. I really couldn't believe her. I mean, how any twelve-year-old could have the confidence to wear skimpy, slinky dresses was beyond me. Then again, Samara was no normal twelve-year-old.

We finally managed to get her out of the store.

"So what happened with Parker Marks, anyway?" Darcy asked as we walked along the sidewalk.

"Isn't he a dreamboat?" Samara gushed.

"Is he really a model?" Darcy asked.

"Oh, yes!" Samara said. "In fact, next month they're flying him to Bermuda to do the spring Icarus catalog."

"I sure hope he doesn't get too much sun," I quipped.

"Why not?" Samara asked with a scowl. "I think he looks great with a tan. Actually, that's where he said he had to go after the game."

"Bermuda?" I asked with a scowl.

"No, the tanning place," my stepsister said. "He

said he has to go four times a week in order to maintain a tan all winter long. It takes a lot of discipline."

"I bet," I said, rolling my eyes in disbelief.

"Know what?" Samara stopped and looked around. "That was nearly half an hour ago. He could be finished by now. Maybe we should go find him."

"Don't even think about it, Samara," I said.

"Why not?" she asked.

"Well, for one thing, it's starting to get dark and we have to walk home," I said. "For another, he's not going to like you if you keep chasing him around."

"Why not?" Samara asked.

"Because boys don't like that," I said.

Samara wrinkled her nose at me. "You're totally old-fashioned, Kit."

"Not true," I said.

"Yes, you are," Samara said. "It's different now. I mean, isn't that what being politically correct is about?"

Darcy and I gave each other knowing smiles. It was hard to imagine Samara being adorable. But this was one of those rare moments when she almost came close.

"Okay," I said. "Let me rephrase that. Boys *do* like it when girls chase them. I mean, I'm sure that deep down inside Chance loves it when all these girls call and send him things. The problem is, he doesn't like any of them. At least, not in a romantic kind of way."

"How do you know?" Samara asked.

"I know because he tells me," I said. "The way to get a boy to like you is to get him to notice you. You have to make him think that you're hard to get and that it will be a challenge to win you over."

"It's like video games," Darcy said.

"Video games?" Samara repeated in a bewildered tone.

"Sure," said Darcy as we walked along the sidewalk. "Every week my little brother gets a new game. He plays it all week and by the weekend he's beaten it. Then it goes into a pile, and he never plays it again."

"I see," Samara said thoughtfully. "There's just one problem. If I don't let Parker Marks know I'm interested in him, when will I ever see him again?"

"You'll just have to find an opportunity," I said as we came around a corner.

"Uh-oh." Darcy stopped.

Ahead of us on the sidewalk was a crowd of kids. I recognized the boys from the dress shop among them, but there were even more now.

One of the boys was pointing at us and saying something. I couldn't hear what he was saying, but then, I didn't really have to.

It was obvious that we were in big trouble.

Next to me Darcy swallowed nervously. "I hate to say this, guys, but it's time to run!"

Chapter 7

We started to run. The boys started to follow. My first thought was to head back toward town and seek safety in a store. But when I looked back over my shoulder, I saw that some of the boys in the group had split off from the others.

"Not that way!" I yelled as we came to another corner.

"But that's toward town," Darcy said.

"I know that," I said, "and so do they. Some of them are going to try to cut us off."

"You really don't think they'll hurt us, do you?" Samara asked, breathing hard.

"You want to stop and ask?" I shot back.

"No, thanks!"

"Let's go this way." I turned and headed toward Marview Park, the large public park that separated our two towns.

It was almost dark now and the park was deserted. The gang of boys behind us was catching up. We ran past the tennis courts and across a grassy field.

"Get 'em! They're from Soundview!" the boys yelled as they ran. They were getting closer!

Suddenly I skidded to a stop. There was a chain-link fence in front of us! Because it was getting dark, I hadn't seen it from a distance. I looked to the right and left, but the fence appeared to wrap around us on both sides.

It was a backstop to a baseball field!

Darcy and Samara had stopped beside me. There was no place left to go. The backstop blocked us on three sides. We turned and faced the crowd of boys.

They stopped a dozen yards away. For a moment, we all just stood there, breathing too hard to speak. But finally I found my voice. I was trembling inside and very afraid. My stomach was in knots, and my heart was beating so hard it hurt.

"Okay," I said. "You've chased us into the park and caught us. What are you going to do now? Beat up three girls?"

The boys glanced at one another uncertainly. I had a feeling that they were just mad about their team being beaten by Soundview. And that they hadn't really stopped to think about why they were chasing us.

But then one of the boys stepped forward. "Maybe we will."

"Well, that's really brave," I said. "Beating up three defenseless girls."

"Maybe we don't care," said another one of the boys.

Yet another boy bent down and picked something up from the ground. "Or maybe we'll just throw rocks at you."

Now the other boys started to pick up rocks.

Things were looking very, very bad.

"I wouldn't do that if I were you," someone behind the crowd of boys said.

I looked past them and couldn't believe what I was seeing. It was Heavenly!

The boys turned and stared at her. She was wearing her baggy brown sweater and bright red scarf.

"Who're you?" one of them asked.

"It doesn't matter who I am," Heavenly answered.

"I know who you are," said one of the boys. "I remember you from the game. You're, like, a baby-sitter or something."

"That's right," Heavenly said calmly. "I'm like a baby-sitter or something. Now I suggest you put down the rocks and go."

"Or what?" asked one of the boys with a laugh. "What are you gonna do, baby-sitter? Take us all on?"

The other boys started to laugh.

"Yeah!" yelled one of the boys. "Why don't we throw some rocks at the baby-sitter, too?"

It was starting to look *worse* than very bad. Some of the boys holding rocks brought their arms back as if they were about to throw. But Heavenly didn't budge. Instead she reached toward her left ear and seemed to rub it.

"I know you're all angry that Marwich lost the soccer game," Heavenly said. "But that's not these girls' fault and it's not my fault. I think it would be a mistake to throw those rocks. I think you'd be wise to put them down."

No one moved. Heavenly's words hung in the air. I doubted the boys would change their minds. Why should they?

But to my absolute amazement, the boys who'd had their arms up to throw the rocks began to lower them. I heard tiny thuds as the rocks fell to the ground.

And then something even more amazing happened. Without a word the whole group of boys began to walk away, back toward Marwich.

When they were gone, Heavenly stepped toward us. "Are you three okay?"

Samara, Darcy, and I nodded.

"Good," Heavenly said. "We'd better get home."

We started to walk out of the park. It was almost dark now. Not one of us spoke. I think we were all feeling a strong mixture of shock and relief.

"How did you do that?" I finally asked.

"Do what?" Heavenly replied as if she didn't know what I was talking about.

"You got them to drop their rocks and go away," I said.

"I just appealed to their better nature," Heavenly answered.

"But how did you even know where we were?" I asked.

"Now, that was the lucky part," Heavenly said. "I decided to take a shortcut through the park to look for you in Marwich. The last thing I expected was to find you here."

"Wow," said Darcy. "Then we really were lucky."

Maybe, I couldn't help thinking. *Or maybe it was something more than luck.*

Chapter

I was certain there was more to what happened than Heavenly let on. But I didn't want to say anything in front of Darcy and Samara, so I waited until that night after dinner.

We had pizza for dinner because Heavenly had gone out and looked for us instead of cooking. Dinner took longer than usual because the phone wouldn't stop ringing. People kept calling Chance to congratulate him on the game.

A lot of the callers were girls.

"Wow," Heavenly said after Chance got calls from three girls in a row. "I never knew a boy who got as many calls from girls as you, Chance."

As usual, Chance shrugged as if it was no big deal. Meanwhile, I noticed that Samara was staring at me. Now she turned to Chance.

"Let me ask you something, Chance," she said. "Do you like the girls who call you?"

"Sure," Chance said with a grin. "I like all girls."

"He never met a girl he didn't like," my ten-year-old brother Robby said as he started on his fourth slice of pizza. Robby had played with a friend instead of going to the soccer game.

"Yeah, and you never met a doughnut you didn't like," Chance shot back.

"Seriously, Chance," Samara said. "Would you like them more if they didn't call?"

Chance frowned. "Would I like the girls who call more if they didn't call? I'm not sure that makes sense."

"You know what she means," I said.

"I don't think it matters whether they call or not," Chance said.

"So it doesn't hurt if they call," Samara said, giving me a look as if it proved her point.

"That's not the point," I said and turned to Chance. "Tell the truth, Chance. Are any of the girls who call the ones you really like?"

"What does 'really like' mean?" Chance asked playfully.

"You know," I said. "Really, *really* like. Like romance."

Chance smiled and winked. "Not as much as I like *you*, Kit."

"Ooooooh!" Robby laughed. Even Samara,

who usually had no sense of humor, smiled. I felt my face turn red.

"Look!" Robby cried. "She's blushing!"

"Okay, okay," Heavenly said, getting up from the kitchen table. "That's enough. So, can I assume that dinner's done?"

We all gave each other dismal looks. When Heavenly first came to live with us, she'd made it clear that we would be expected to help do the dishes and clean up the kitchen after dinner each night.

No other nanny had ever made us help around the house, and we'd argued with Heavenly, but she was firm about it, and after a while we just accepted that this was the way life would be.

"I guess so," I said.

"Then I have good news," Heavenly announced. "Since you spent the afternoon watching Chance's soccer match instead of doing homework, I'm going to make an exception tonight. You can all go study. I'll do the dishes."

"All right!" Chance jumped up.

"I'm out of here before someone changes her mind," said Robby as he pushed his chair back.

The two boys hurried out of the kitchen. I decided to stay behind and play with our new puppy. I was hoping that if the others left, I might get a chance to ask Heavenly some questions.

But for some reason, Samara was also slow to leave the kitchen table.

Heavenly gave her a puzzled look. "Want to help clean up, Samara?"

My stepsister shook her head. "Can I ask you a question, Heavenly?"

"I guess."

"Everyone tells me it's wrong to call this boy I know, but I don't see why," she said.

"There's nothing wrong with calling a boy," Heavenly said.

"She's not telling you the whole story," I said as I watched a ladybug crawl across the kitchen table. Again I wondered where in the world they were coming from.

"Oh?" Heavenly raised an eyebrow curiously.

"Well, I like him and I want him to like me," Samara explained. "But Kit says if I call him, he won't like me."

"I don't understand," Heavenly said.

"It's like with Chance," I tried to explain. "All those girls call Chance all the time, but he's never going to fall in love with them. The girl Chance falls in love with is the one who doesn't call."

"How do you know?" Heavenly asked.

"Because it's like Roy and me," I said. "For years I had a huge crush on him. But now that he calls all the time and always wants to be with me, I'm not so sure how I feel."

Heavenly nodded. "I see your point, Kit. But I'm not sure everyone thinks the way you think."

"But if I call Parker Marks, there's a *possibility* he won't like me?" Samara asked miserably.

"It's very hard to say," Heavenly said.

"Let me tell you one thing about Parker Marks," I added. "He's gorgeous. If you think a lot of girls call Chance, then Parker must need a private answering service to take his calls."

Heavenly pursed her lips. "If that's true, Samara, then calling him might not be the best idea."

The corners of Samara's mouth turned down and her eyes grew watery. "But then, how will I ever get to see him again?" she asked with a sniff.

The lines in Heavenly's forehead deepened. "You really like him that much?"

Samara nodded. A tear rolled out of her eye and down her cheek. I have to admit that I was shocked. I'd never seen her act like this before.

"Well, you never know," Heavenly said. "Sometimes when you least expect it, the opportunity comes along."

Samara gave her a hopeful look. "You think?"

"Why don't we wait a day or two and see what happens?" Heavenly said.

"Oh, Heavenly!" Samara jumped out of her chair and ran over and hugged her. "You're the best!"

I couldn't believe what I was seeing. This just

couldn't be the Samara Rand I knew. I got up and put my hand on her forehead.

"What are you doing?" Samara asked.

"Checking to see if you're running a fever," I said.

"Drop dead, twit," Samara snarled and left.

Chapter

"I take it back," I said after Samara left. "She's completely normal."

"No, she's not," Heavenly said with a smile. "She's in love."

"Love?" I frowned. "But she just met Parker Marks today."

"Puppy love," said Heavenly. "Believe me, it doesn't take much the first time."

"You sound like you know," I said.

"Maybe I do," Heavenly replied with a wink.

"I just can't believe it," I said, shaking my head. "Yesterday she didn't even think about boys. Today she can't think about anything else."

"Uh-huh." Heavenly nodded as if that wasn't unusual, either.

"You know," I said, "I really hate to admit this, but I do feel bad for her. I mean, we never go to

Marwich and those kids never come here. If she doesn't call Parker, how will she get to see him again?"

"You never know," Heavenly said.

She was being mysterious again. That reminded me of why I'd stayed in the kitchen playing with our new puppy, who still didn't have a name. He loved to play tug-of-war. He grabbed one end of an old red-and-white dishrag in his mouth. I held on to the other end. Meanwhile, Tyler sat in his high chair playing with a ring of plastic keys, and Heavenly cleaned up.

"Wow, I can't believe how much stronger he is now than he was when we got him a month ago," I said as the puppy and I played.

Heavenly looked over from the sink. "Just wait. He's still a puppy. In a few months you won't even be able to hold on to your end of the rag."

"Then I guess I better have fun with him now," I said.

"Actually, what you should be doing now is your homework," Heavenly reminded me.

"I will. I just wanted to ask you a question," I said. "But I'd really appreciate it if you gave me an honest answer and didn't try to avoid it."

"Uh-oh." Heavenly gave me a smile. "Sounds like trouble."

"Really, Heavenly, I'm serious," I said. "I really want to know how you knew those boys had chased us into the park."

"Is that all?" Heavenly replied. "I told you. I was trying to take a shortcut between Soundview Manor and Marwich."

"I know that's what you said. The trouble is that cutting across the park *isn't* a shortcut. It's actually out of the way."

Heavenly gave me a sheepish smile. "Well, then I guess I was just plain lucky."

"I told you I'm *serious,*" I stressed.

"So am I," she said.

I *knew* she wasn't telling me the truth. Well . . . at least, I was pretty sure she wasn't.

"Okay, let's move on," I said.

"I feel like I'm being questioned by the police," Heavenly said.

"Close," I grumbled. "Now I'd like to know what you did that got all those boys to change their minds, drop their rocks, and walk away."

"Why, that's a simple one," Heavenly said. "I cast a spell on them."

I felt my jaw drop in total surprise. "You actually admit it?"

Heavenly winked. "Well, that *is* what you wanted me to say, isn't it?"

"I . . . I wanted you to tell me the truth," I sputtered. "Is that the truth?"

"In a way." Heavenly cocked her head to the side thoughtfully. "I suppose you could say I cast a spell of common sense over them."

Here we go, I thought.

"I mean, it wouldn't do them any good to throw stones at us, would it?" Heavenly went on.

"That's not what I'm talking about," I said.

"And it certainly wouldn't do *us* any good," Heavenly continued. "I mean, getting hit by those rocks and all."

"Stop it!" I shouted.

The puppy yelped with surprise.

Tyler jumped and dropped his plastic keys on the floor. His eyes grew wide and he started to cry.

"Oh, gosh, I'm sorry," I said.

"It's okay. It's time for him to go to bed anyway." Heavenly went over and picked Tyler up. "You got scared, huh?"

Tyler nodded and rubbed his eyes with his pudgy little fists. I also got up and went over to him.

"I'm sorry, Ty," I said, stroking his head.

"We can talk about this another time," Heavenly said. "I'll put him to bed. Since you don't seem to have much homework, would you finish up in the kitchen?"

"Sure."

Heavenly left and I took the sponge and started to wipe down the kitchen counter. But all I felt was frustration. Once again, Heavenly had escaped.

Chapter

10

The next morning when we got to school, there were two Soundview Manor police cars in the middle school parking lot, plus vans from two of the local television stations.

"What's going on?" Robby asked. As usual, Chance had already gone off with his friends to the high school.

"I don't know," said Heavenly.

"Let's go see," Robby said.

"No, you have to go into school," Heavenly said, and pointed at the elementary building. "We'll tell you later."

"That's not fair!" Robby complained. "You guys are gonna go over there and find out right now."

"I have a feeling you'll find out just as soon as you get into school," Heavenly assured him. "Now get going."

Robby went into the elementary school and the rest of us headed toward the middle school. As we got closer, I began to notice long streaks of black-and-orange paint on the windows and outside walls of the school. Janitors were scrubbing the paint off the brick and scraping it off the windows with razor blades.

"Looks like Marwich got their revenge after all," Heavenly said.

"Can you believe it?" Samara asked.

"I'm afraid so," said Heavenly as she stopped the stroller. "You two have a good day in school, and I'll see you this afternoon."

Heavenly turned the stroller around and headed back toward home. Samara and I headed into school.

"This is bad," Samara said with a pout.

"You mean, the damage?" I guessed.

"No, I mean for Parker," Samara said. "If kids around here know who he is, then he'll never be able to come to Soundview Manor. Everyone's going to be so angry at those Marwich kids for doing this."

"I'm glad to see you care so much about our school," I said sarcastically.

Samara looked at me and pushed out her lower lip. I was amazed to see her eyes start to fill with tears. "You just don't understand anything, Kit!"

The next thing I knew, she ran into school ahead of me. I still couldn't believe the transformation in my stepsister. Maybe she was right. Maybe I didn't understand.

That day in school all anyone could talk about was what Marwich had done.

"They're just really bad sports," Roy said at lunch.

"I heard that some boys from our school are going to paint their school blue and white tonight," Darcy said.

"Oh, great," I muttered. "An all-out paint war! That's just what we need!"

"I bet the paint store in town won't mind," Roy said with a smile. "They could sell a lot of paint."

"So how's Samara?" Darcy asked.

"Still in love," I said.

"Ah, young love!" Roy put his hands over his heart and let out a big fake sigh.

"Roy, let me ask you a question," I said. "What do you think of girls calling boys?"

Roy let out another big sigh. Only this time it was real. "I don't know, Kit, it's not something that happens to me a lot."

"But suppose it did," I said.

Roy got a funny gleam in his eye. "From any girl in particular?"

"A girl who liked you," I said.

"Is she sitting at this table?" Roy asked hopefully.

I had to smile. "You're sweet, Roy."

But to my surprise, Roy frowned. "Don't call me sweet, Kit. Please?"

"Why not?" I asked.

"Because sweet boys are the ones girls like to tell their love troubles to," Roy said.

"Okay," I said. "Suppose I call you cute."

"No way." Roy shook his head. "Cute boys are the ones whose shoulders girls cry on when their hearts get broken by the boys they *really* like."

"Then what should I call you?" I asked.

"How about ruggedly handsome?" Roy suggested. "Or stud. Or better yet, my main man!"

"Let's get back to the subject," I said. "We were talking about girls calling boys."

"Not exactly," Roy pointed out. "You're talking about a girl from Soundview Manor calling a boy from Marwich."

"Right."

Roy shook his head. "You know Romeo and Juliet? They were in love, but their families totally hated each other. Well, I have news for you. Right now that's nothing compared to the way our two towns feel."

"So you're saying it's hopeless?" Darcy asked.

"I'm saying, if I were you, I'd get your stepsister a dog," Roy said.

"We already have a dog," I pointed out.

"Then a cat," Roy said.

"We have one of those, too," I said.

Roy scratched his head. "How does she feel about hamsters?"

Chapter

11

That afternoon we all did our homework at the kitchen table as usual. We usually got an hour of free time before dinner, and as soon as that time came, Robby and Samara would head for the big TV in the living room.

But today Samara was nowhere in sight. I stayed in the kitchen for an extra few minutes just to finish up some math homework.

"Where is she?" I asked Heavenly, who was sitting at the kitchen table drawing with Tyler.

"In her room," Heavenly answered.

"Why?"

"Heartbroken. Miserable. No appetite. No desire to do anything except stare at the walls."

"Wow, I can't believe this," I said.

"I know," Heavenly said. "It's sad."

"It's worse than sad," I said. "It's hopeless. You

should have seen the kids at school today. Everyone in Marwich hates Soundview because we beat them in soccer. And now everyone in Soundview hates Marwich because they painted all over our school. Even if Samara saw Parker again, it wouldn't work. She can't go there and he can't come here."

Heavenly pursed her lips and stared off. "It's really not fair," she said, more to herself than to me.

There didn't seem to be anything more to say, so I looked back down at my math homework. I was working on a problem when out of the corner of my eye I noticed a bright red ladybug crawling along the kitchen table.

Suddenly the ladybug stopped crawling and became very still. That wasn't unusual, but what happened next was *very* unusual. Was it my imagination, or did the ladybug start to glow?

I started to raise my head, but then caught myself. If something strange was going on, I didn't want Heavenly to see that I was aware of it. I looked back down at my math homework, but out of the corner of my eye, I watched Heavenly.

Her eyes were closed, and she had stopped drawing. She was touching her left ear with her left hand and her lips were moving.

"Hey, everyone!" Robby suddenly yelled from the living room. "You have to see this!"

Heavenly's eyes burst open unexpectedly. For a moment we just stared at each other. Heavenly's eyes went wide.

"Come on!" Robby yelled. "I mean it! You have to see this!"

We all hurried into the living room. Robby was staring at the TV. On the screen was an image of our school.

"This, I really don't believe!" Robby gasped. A dark-haired reporter was standing in front of the school holding a microphone as she spoke to the camera:

"School officials were dismayed this morning to discover this latest incident of vandalism, which came last night after a soccer game between Soundview Manor and Marwich middle schools," the reporter said. *"And here with me is Principal Leslie Jones of the Soundview Manor Middle School."*

"Oh, wow!" I said as the TV camera turned to our principal. "It's Principal Jones!"

Samara and Chance hurried into the living room.

"What's going on?" Chance asked.

"Check it out," Robby said. "We're famous!"

On the TV the reporter held her microphone up to Principal Jones's face. *"Isn't it true that tensions between your district and Marwich have always run high?"*

"I wouldn't call them tensions," Principal Jones replied. *"Our two districts have simply enjoyed a long and healthy rivalry for a long time."*

"But vandalism was never part of that rivalry before, was it?" asked the reporter.

"Not in my memory," replied Principal Jones.

"Have there been any talks about what the two districts can do to prevent future vandalism?" the reporter asked.

"As a matter of fact, I've just gotten off the phone with Principal Petersen from Marwich Middle School, and we have decided to do something about it," Principal Jones replied. "Since the students in our schools will be facing each other many times in many different sports during the next half dozen years, we've decided to come up with a way for them to get to know each other better."

"So it's your feeling that if the students get to know each other better and maybe even become friends, it will foster the feeling of competition without the vandalism?" the reporter guessed.

"They're going to try to get Soundview and Marwich to be friends?" Chance asked with a chuckle. "This should be good."

On the TV, Principal Jones nodded. "Yes, we've agreed on a series of activities designed to bring the students of our two schools together so they can get to know each other."

"Can you give us an example?" asked the reporter.

"Certainly," said Principal Jones. "We intend to start next Friday night with a dance to which both schools will be invited."

"A dance?" Chance said.

"It's not such a bad idea," said Heavenly. "What do you think, Kit?"

I couldn't say I was thrilled. All I could think about was dancing with Roy. I had no idea whether he was a good dancer or not. All I knew was that he was shorter than I am. I have to admit that his height (or lack of it) did bother me a little. But I knew that at a dance it would bother me a lot.

"What do you think, Samara?" Heavenly asked.

At the mention of Samara's name, I realized that I hadn't heard a peep from my stepsister since the newscast began. We all looked over at her. She was sitting almost perfectly still, staring at the TV with a stunned expression on her face.

"Did she say a dance?" She sounded stunned.

"Yes," said Robby. "What's the big deal?"

Samara sank back into the couch with a dreamy look on her face. "Parker Marks," she said.

Chapter

12

"Don't you think I'm going to look fantastic?" Samara asked.

It was a week later, the night before the dance. Samara was standing on a stool in the kitchen wearing her brand-new red dress. It was the incredibly expensive low-cut one she'd tried on at that store in Marwich. True to her word, Samara had gotten Mom to buy it for her.

Heavenly was kneeling in front of her, pinning up the dress's hem.

"Have you ever heard of the word *modesty*?" I asked. I was sitting at the kitchen table, doing my homework.

Samara wrinkled her nose at me. "I'm just being honest. I can't help if it this dress makes me look wicked fabulous."

"That dress may make you look wicked fabulous," I said, "but I think you're going to feel wicked *dumb* wearing it to the dance. Everyone else is going to be wearing normal clothes."

Samara nodded. "Exactly."

"Exactly what?" I asked.

"Everyone else is going to look completely uninteresting," Samara said. "While I will be truly unique."

"You're unique, all right," I grumbled.

Heavenly turned and winked at me. She had time to help Samara with the dress because Tyler was taking a nap. The puppy was chewing on a rawhide bone on the kitchen floor.

"You're just jealous," Samara said with a huff.

"Jealous of what?" I asked.

Samara pressed her lips together and frowned, but didn't answer.

"Come on, Samara," I said, "I'm dying to find out what I'm jealous of."

"That you don't have a boyfriend like Parker Marks," she said.

"I have news for you, Samara," I said. "You don't have a boyfriend like Parker Marks, either. You don't even know if he's going to the dance."

"He'll be there," Samara said.

"How do you know?" I asked. "Have you spoken to him?"

Samara shook her head. "I just know it," she snapped irritably. "He *will* be there! He *has* to be there."

Grrrrrrrr. I heard a tiny growl and felt something tugging on my leg. I looked under the kitchen table. The puppy had my shoelace in his mouth and was playing tug-of-war with it.

"Don't you think it's time we gave him a name?" I said. "He's been here for more than a month already."

"I gave him a name, but nobody liked it," Samara said.

"Nobody calls their dogs Lassie anymore," I said.

"I don't see why not," Samara said.

"For the same reason twelve-year-old girls don't wear slinky red dresses to dances," I said.

"You'll see." Samara turned up her nose. "I'll be the queen of the scene."

"The laughingstock is more like it," I muttered.

"That's enough, Kit," Heavenly said sternly. "I happen to think that Samara's very brave to wear a dress. There's nothing wrong with being a little different. It would be pretty boring if we were all the same."

I can't say I was surprised to hear Heavenly say that. After all, she was the only nanny in town with spiky purple hair, a pierced eyebrow, and tattoos.

"I was only trying to do you a favor," I told Samara. "I'm warning you that if you wear that dress tomorrow night, you're going to be miserable."

"Everyone's going to be miserable tomorrow night," said Robby as he came into the kitchen.

"Why?" asked Heavenly.

"Because there's a big storm headed this way," Robby reported. "I just read about it on the Internet. There's going to be wet snow, sleet, freezing rain, and winds up to seventy miles an hour."

"Uh-oh," I muttered. "You know what that means."

"Get out the candles and flashlights," said Robby.

"You're such pessimists," Samara complained. "Just because there's freezing rain and wind doesn't mean we're going to lose our electricity."

"True," I said. "But you have to admit that it happens an awful lot."

The problem with Soundview Manor was that it was old and the electric lines ran along the telephone poles. The town also had lots of big old trees. Freezing rain and sleet meant that the branches would get weighed down with ice. That alone was usually enough to make branches snap and fall on the electric lines. But when you added seventy-mile-an-hour winds, it was time to stock up on food and make sure you had lots of flashlights and warm clothes around.

"Where are Mom and Dad?" Robby asked.

Heavenly went over to the big calendar where we kept track of our parents' movements.

"Your dad's in Korea until next Thursday,"

Heavenly reported. "Your mom's due back from Italy on Saturday night."

"That's not going to help," said Robby.

"We'll be just fine," Heavenly said. "We've got plenty of food and clothes. You know, there was a time once when the only heat houses had around here came from burning coal."

"How do you know?" I asked.

"Oh, uh, that's the way houses *everywhere* used to be heated," Heavenly replied.

Heavenly seemed to know an awful lot about the history of Soundview Manor.

"The dance can't be canceled," Samara said, biting her lip. "It just can't!"

"Why not?" Robby asked.

"Because Parker's going to be there, and I'm going to look so great," Samara said.

"Oh, please!" I groaned.

"It's true!" my stepsister insisted. "Besides, I made Mom spend a fortune on this dress."

"So, can't you save it for the next dance?" Robby asked.

Samara shook her head. "It might be out of style by then."

"I have news for you," I said. "It's out of style *now.*"

Samara made a face. "You're *so* not funny, Kit."

From the front hall came the ding-dong of the doorbell.

"It's Wes," I said, watching Heavenly closely to

see how she reacted. Wesley Shackelford was our piano teacher. I was pretty sure he had a crush on Heavenly, but it was hard to tell how she felt about him.

"Is someone going to let him in?" Heavenly asked.

"Samara should," said Robby. "Wes always likes to get her lesson out of the way first."

"Do I have to?" Samara whined.

"You know your mom wants you to take your lessons," Heavenly said.

"But I didn't practice once this week," Samara said.

"So what else is new?" Robby asked with a grin.

Samara wrinkled her nose at him. "You think you're so smart."

"I think you should go just to see what he thinks of your dress," I said.

"Wes wouldn't say a thing," Samara countered. "He's much too well brought up. He has manners. Unlike *you.*"

"He may have manners," I shot back, "but that won't stop him from barfing."

"Kit!" Heavenly said sternly. "That's *enough!*"

Samara stuck her tongue out at me and left the kitchen.

"I think you're being a little mean," Heavenly said after my stepsister had gone.

"She asks for it," I replied. "She's so full of herself. She really thinks she's the most beautiful girl in the world."

"The rest of us know that's not true," Heavenly said. "So what does it matter?"

"I don't know," I replied with a shrug. "It just bothers me."

The phone rang. Heavenly answered it, then held it out to me. "It's Roy."

I took the phone. Our new puppy chased my shoelace across the kitchen and started tugging on it again, until I shooed him away.

"Hello?" I said.

"Hi, Kit," Roy said.

"Hi, Roy," I replied. "What's up?"

"You know the dance tomorrow night?" he asked.

"Please, don't remind me," I groaned, thinking of Samara and her dress.

"Huh?" Roy sounded confused.

"Nothing," I said. "What about it?"

"The word is that the only kids who are really serious about going are the sixth graders," Roy said. "The seventh and eighth graders have pretty much decided it's totally uncool."

"Phew!" I heaved a sigh of relief.

"Here's the bad news," Roy went on. "Principal Jones cornered me in the hall today and got me to promise to work at the refreshment table. So, uh, I was wondering if you'd like to work there with me."

I have to admit that my first reaction was not one of great enthusiasm. The idea of pouring soda for a bunch of giddy, goofy sixth graders was about the last thing in the world I wanted to do.

"I know what you're thinking, Kit," Roy said. "It's a total drag. But if the two of us did it together, it might not be so bad. Come on, want to do it?"

"Well . . ." I hesitated and glanced around. A bright red ladybug was crawling across the kitchen ceiling.

"It could actually be fun," Roy said. "We'll have all the free soda we want, and we'll get to watch the sixth graders make fools of themselves on the dance floor."

"Sounds like a great time," I grumbled.

"It will be!" Roy insisted. "You have to believe me. Come on, Kit, don't say no."

It was pretty obvious that Roy really wanted me to do it. But then again, Roy called almost every night with something he really wanted me to do. And I couldn't do everything, could I?

I was just about to thank Roy for the invitation, but add that I had other plans. Then I realized that if I did work at the dance, I'd be able to watch Samara with Parker Marks. That was, *if* Parker actually showed up. That alone would probably be worth it.

"Okay, I will," I said.

I don't think Roy heard me because he said, "Oh, come on, Kit. This'll really be fun. I promise."

"I said I'd do it, Roy."

"I know, but . . ." There was a moment of silence on the phone. "Uh, what did you say?"

"I said I'll work at the refreshment table with you."

"You did? You will? Oh, wow, that's great, Kit! I promise you won't be sorry."

The kitchen door opened and Chance came in. He swept his light brown hair off his forehead and fixed me with his piercing blue eyes. Then he turned to Heavenly.

"Let me guess," he said. "She's talking to Roy Chandler."

Heavenly nodded. Meanwhile, on the phone, Roy was still assuring me that I'd have a great time pouring soda for sixth graders at the dance.

"Doesn't that kid have anything better to do than bother you all the time?" Chance asked loudly with a devilish grin. I knew at once that he was hoping Roy would hear him.

"Huh?" Roy said on the phone. "Did someone say something?"

I shook my fist at Chance and then quickly turned back to the phone. "Uh, it was nothing, Roy. I'll see you in school tomorrow, and we'll talk about it then."

Roy must've sensed that I was about to hang up, because he cried, "Wait!"

"Now what?" I asked.

On the other side of the kitchen Chance opened the refrigerator. "You know what I don't understand?" he said loudly. "Why Kit even bothers with these eighth-grade dweebs. She should be going out with older guys."

"Did someone say something about a dweeb?" Roy asked over the phone.

"Just a second, Roy." I clamped my hand over the phone and once again shook my fist at Chance. Then I turned to Heavenly. "Can't you stop him?"

Heavenly nodded and turned to Chance. "She's right. You're embarrassing her."

Chance made a big fake pout but didn't say anything more. I took my hand off the phone. "Sorry, Roy, some big jerk was bothering me. Now, what were you saying?"

"Uh, just that I thought I should make arrangements to pick you up at your house before the dance."

"You don't have to do that," I said. "I can get there myself."

"No, no, I insist," Roy said. "We have to go early to set up. It's the least I can do."

I knew that it was silly for Roy to pick me up and take me to the dance. But I also knew that he wouldn't take no for an answer. And the longer I stayed on the phone with him, the more likely Chance would say something loud and embarrassing again.

"All right," I said. "I'll see you here tomorrow night, and then we'll go over to school."

"Great!" Roy said. "Really, Kit, you won't be sorry."

We'll see about that, I thought. Then I said good-bye and hung up.

"Wow," Chance said with a grin. "You mean he actually let you get off the phone?"

"Would you mind telling me what your problem is?" I shot back.

Chapter

13

I don't have a problem," Chance answered.

"Why do you keep bothering me while I'm on the phone?" I asked.

"I just don't understand why you put up with that eighth-grade twerp," Chance said.

"Maybe because I'm also in eighth grade," I replied. "And the boy you're calling a twerp happens to be a friend of mine."

"A friend?" Chance laughed. "I hate to tell you this, Kit, but that kid's totally head over heels in love with you."

I rolled my eyes. "What business is it of yours?"

"Forget it, Kit." Chance shrugged and started out of the kitchen. "I just think you're wasting your time when you could be going out with older guys."

"Like who?" I asked.

But Chance didn't answer. The kitchen door swung closed. He was gone.

I turned to Heavenly. "Would someone please tell me what's going on?"

Heavenly didn't answer. She just smiled as if she knew the answer but didn't want to say.

"I think he's jealous," Robby piped up.

"Of who?" I asked.

"Roy," said Robby.

"Why?" I asked.

"Haven't you been listening to him lately?" Robby asked. "He's always talking about how good you look. I mean, I'm just a fourth-grade turbo geek, and it's even obvious to me."

"But he's my stepbrother," I said.

"So?" said Robby.

"It's weird," I said. "I—" I was about to explain why I thought it was weird when something else caught my attention. Our new puppy was now following something across the kitchen floor. I looked closer and saw that it was a ladybug. The puppy kept trying to pounce on it, but each time he did, the ladybug would fly just out of reach and then land again.

I looked up at the kitchen ceiling. The other ladybug was still up there.

"Where are all these ladybugs coming from?" I asked.

"What ladybugs?" Robby asked.

"The one on the ceiling and the one on the floor that the puppy is chasing."

Robby looked at the ceiling and then at the floor. "It's a strange time of year for ladybugs, isn't it?"

I glanced over at Heavenly, but she quickly looked away.

"It's a strange time of year for a lot of things," I said. "Don't pretend you don't know about this, Heavenly. You know that I think you're the best nanny who's ever worked here, but a lot of strange things have happened since you came."

As always, Heavenly pretended to be innocent. "I don't know what you're talking about."

"I'm talking about soda cans that won't open when you don't want someone to drink soda, and doorknobs that come off doors when you don't want someone to leave the house. I'm talking about boys who never paid any attention to me and now suddenly won't leave me alone. I'm talking about ladybugs. I'm talking about gangs of boys suddenly deciding not to throw rocks at us. I'm talking about Principal Jones suddenly deciding our school should have a dance with our archenemy Marwich."

"Why do you think I had anything to do with that?" Heavenly asked.

"Because all those things happened since you got here," I said.

"If there was an earthquake, would that mean I caused it, too?" she asked.

"That's not the same thing," I argued.

Heavenly didn't answer. Her eyes darted toward the yellow-and-blue plastic baby monitor perched on the kitchen counter. I thought I heard the faint sound of rustling come from the monitor, but I wasn't sure.

"Sounds like Mr. Wiggler's up," Heavenly said. She started to get up.

"I can't believe you heard that," I said. "I barely heard anything."

Heavenly smiled. "It's my job to hear him." She left the kitchen and headed upstairs to get Tyler. From the living room came the jarring, off-key sounds of Samara playing the piano.

I looked at Robby. It seemed like once again Heavenly had avoided my questions. "I don't know, Robby," I said. "I mean, I really like Heavenly a lot and I'd never want her to go. But I still think there's something strange about her."

"So do I," said Robby.

"You do?" I asked, surprised.

"Yes," said my brother. "I think she's a Wiccan."

Chapter

14

A what?" I asked.

"It's like a witch, only nicer," Robby explained very matter-of-factly. "Like a sorceress or lady wizard. They only do nice magic."

I gave him an uncertain look. It wasn't that I disagreed. It was just that the way he said it seemed to imply that he didn't think there was anything unusual about it.

"What makes you think that?"

"The same things you talked about before," Robby answered. "It's all spells and charms and stuff. I mean, like the way she just appeared out of nowhere. And how she could always get into the house no matter what we changed the security code to. And how that other nanny Mom and Dad hired to replace her suddenly disappeared. She's a Wiccan, all right."

"How do you know?" I asked.

"I see them all the time in my video games," Robby explained. "Wiccans, sorcerers, sorceresses, wizards, witches. They all do pretty much the same stuff. Only some are good and some are evil."

"You're really serious?" I asked.

"Oh, yeah."

"Aren't you scared?" I asked.

"Of Heavenly? Naw, she seems too nice. She doesn't seem like the type who'd turn one of us into a slug or an earthworm or anything. Although it would be kind of nice if she did it to Samara."

"But if she's really a sorceress, why won't she admit it?" I asked.

"They're not supposed to," Robby said. "It's like a rule or something."

I just kept staring at him. "Robby, do you know what you're saying? You're saying that she can do magic."

"Yeah."

"Well, shouldn't we do something about it?" I asked.

Robby frowned. "Like what?"

"Like get her to admit it," I said. "Or get her to show us how she does it."

"I guess we could," Robby said.

"How?" I asked.

"Well . . ." Robby scratched the side of his nose and thought. "I guess we'd have to set a trap."

"A trap!" I gasped.

"Shhhh!" Robby pressed his finger to his lips. "Don't let her hear you."

"But she's upstairs," I whispered.

"If she's a Wiccan, she can hear from anywhere," Robby whispered back.

"You think?" I asked uncertainly.

"Listen," Robby said. "Did you hear anything from that baby monitor before?"

"Not really. I mean, I wasn't sure."

"See?" Robby said, as if that proved his point.

"So what kind of trap would we set?" I asked.

"Something that'll force Heavenly to reveal her magic powers," Robby said.

"For instance?"

Robby scratched his head. "We could take one of Mom's favorite antiques and drop it out the third-floor window. If Heavenly stops it from breaking, that's proof that she's magical."

"And if she doesn't stop it from breaking?" I pointed out.

"Mom'll throw a fit. Good point."

"Suppose we leave the milk out all night and it goes sour," I proposed. "In the morning there'll be no milk."

"So Heavenly will go to the store and get some," Robby said.

"Right, bad suggestion," I admitted.

For a moment both Robby and I were quiet as we tried to come up with a way to trap Heavenly and make her reveal her magic powers. Meanwhile, the sound of Samara's terrible piano playing drifted in from the living room.

"Talk about magic," I said. "Wouldn't it be great if we could get Heavenly to turn Samara into a good piano player so we didn't have to listen to her awful mistakes?"

"Fat chance," Robby grumbled. "And too bad. Wouldn't it be cool if we could do something to her?"

"Like what?" I asked.

Robby glanced around the kitchen. Suddenly he sat up and blinked. "I know! Her dress!"

"What about it?" I asked.

"Just before the dance tomorrow night, we'll hide it," Robby said. "Samara will throw a fit. Heavenly will tell her to wear a different dress, but you know Samara. She'll act like it's the end of the world. Like life will end if she can't wear *that* dress. I bet you anything Heavenly'll feel so bad for her that she'll make a new replacement dress appear somehow."

"*If* she can do magic," I reminded him. "What if she can't?"

"So Samara doesn't get to wear her dumb dress," Robby said. "Who cares?"

"Don't you think that's a little mean?" I asked.

Just then the kitchen door swung open and Samara pranced in. "Did you listen?" she asked excitedly.

"To what?" Robby asked.

"Me playing," Samara said. "Didn't you hear it? It was the best I've ever done."

"That's not saying much," Robby mumbled.

Samara wrinkled her nose. "You're so jealous, Robby. Just because you have to practice all the time and I don't."

"Why don't you have to practice?" I asked her.

"Because I've got talent," Samara announced.

Robby gave me a weary look and rolled his eyes. I have to admit that I was getting pretty sick of Samara's attitude, too. Maybe she did deserve to have her new dress hidden.

Chapter 15

It was time for me to go out into the living room and take my lesson with Wes. Wes's real name was Wesley Percifal Shackelford III, and he came from the very rich Shackelford family. The Shackelfords owned the Shackelford Semi-conductor Company, which made parts for computers.

But for some reason Wes didn't want anything to do with his family's company. Instead, he wanted to teach piano.

Wes was a very nice man with blond hair. He wasn't exactly handsome, but he was very sweet. Ever since Heavenly arrived in our house, it had been painfully obvious to all of us that Wes had a crush on her. We could tell by the longing gazes he sent in her direction whenever she passed through the living room. The problem was that

Wes was incredibly shy and always started to stammer when he got nervous.

And Heavenly was no help, either. No matter how many hints we dropped, she refused to give us any indication of how she felt about Wes.

I went out to the living room and sat down at the piano bench.

"So, Wes," I said. "What did you think of Samara's dress?"

Was scowled at me. "I don't understand."

"Didn't you just give Samara a piano lesson?" I asked.

"Well, I *tried* to," Wes replied. "I'm still looking forward to the day when she actually practices."

"Don't hold your breath," I said. "Did you notice that she was wearing a tight, low-cut red dress?"

Wes gave me a blank look, then shook his head.

"Men," I muttered. "Okay, forget it."

We started the lesson. Wes always seemed a little nervous, but today he seemed even more nervous than usual. Usually he would ask if I'd been practicing, and he wouldn't ask about Heavenly until practically the end of the lesson. But today I'd only played for a minute before he started in.

"Heavenly's . . . still . . . working here, isn't she?" he asked. This was not an odd question since most of the nannies our parents hired didn't stay with us very long.

"Didn't you see her before?" I asked. "She went upstairs to check on Tyler."

"I must have missed her," Wes said. "How's it, er . . ."

"Going?" I guessed.

Wes nodded.

"Pretty good. She's definitely the best nanny we've ever had."

"Then you think she'll, er . . ."

"Stay?" I guessed.

Wes nodded.

"I hope so," I said.

Wes smiled. You could see that he hoped so, too. I kept waiting for him to continue our piano lesson, but he seemed to have something else on his mind.

"You know about the dance tomorrow night?" he asked.

"Funny you should ask," I said. "I'm going."

"Really?" Wes's eyebrows rose. "Do you have a date?"

"Not exactly. A friend of mine is working at the refreshment table, and he wants me to work with him," I explained.

"Good, then I'll see you there," Wes said.

"You're going?" I asked, surprised.

Wes nodded. "I'm the DJ."

"No way!" I cried.

"Yes, way." Wes said and smiled proudly. "It's going to be my new business. I'm calling myself DJ

Wes and I'm available for dances, birthday parties, weddings, and all other social and business events."

"But what about teaching piano?" I asked.

"I'll still do that," Wes explained. "I mean, unless someone wants me to DJ on a weekday afternoon. But it's kind of doubtful."

"Right," I said. "That's so cool, Wes. I can't wait to hear you."

"There's just one problem," he said.

"What's that?" I asked.

"You know how DJs always have dancers that come along and get everyone to dance?" he asked. "So that everyone doesn't just stand around looking nervous?"

"Sure," I said. "They're professional dancers."

"Well, uh, would you know where I could get one?" Wes asked.

"A professional dancer?" I said. "I wouldn't have a clue."

Wes rubbed his chin. He had a big chin, so there was a lot to rub. "I guess I could look in the Yellow Pages."

"I hate to say this, Wes," I said, "but I think you're a little late for that. The dance is tomorrow night."

"And with my luck, I'd wind up hiring a ballerina," Wes moped.

"Wait!" Suddenly I had a great idea. "You should ask Heavenly. She's a great dancer!"

Wes's eyes widened. "Really?"

"The best," I said. "She's totally wild."

"How wild?" Wes asked a little nervously.

"Wild enough that when my parents saw her dancing, they wanted to fire her," I said.

Wes grinned. "Now, *that's* a good recommendation."

"As soon as everyone sees her dancing, I guarantee you they'll be dancing, too," I said.

"Perfect," Wes said.

"Great," I said.

"Excellent," said Wes.

"Dynamite," I said.

We grinned at each other.

Then Wes's smile sort of faded. "There's, er . . . just one . . . thing."

"What?"

"Could you, er . . ."

"Could I, er, what?" I asked.

"Ask?"

"Ask Heavenly?"

Wes nodded.

"Of course I could," I said. "But don't you think you should?"

Wes shook his head. I could see that he was feeling nervous and shy again.

"But it doesn't make sense," I said. "You're going to have to talk to her at some point. I mean, if you're going to work together tomorrow night."

Wes winced at the thought.

"Come on, Wes," I said. "How did you think you'd communicate with her? Hand signals?"

Wes's shoulders seemed to slump in defeat. "I guess I really didn't think about it."

"Well, now's the time to think of it," I said.

Wes's eyes went wide . . . with terror.

"Come on," I said. "You're a grown-up guy, and she's a grown-up girl. And it's not like you're asking her out on a date. You're offering her a job. She'll make some money, won't she?"

"Oh, definitely," Wes said.

"Then she'll probably really appreciate it."

Wes glanced nervously at the kitchen door. As I've said before, Wes wasn't a bad-looking guy. His nose was a little too big, and his eyes were set a shade too deep. But it wasn't like Heavenly was a supermodel, either. I actually thought they'd make a nice couple.

"So what do you say?" I asked.

Wes shook his head mutely. He was still too nervous.

My piano teacher may have been nearly twice my age, but he was one of those people you could talk to. I put my hand on his shoulder and gave him a serious look.

"Listen, Wes," I said, "Heavenly is a really, really nice person. And a really sensitive person. I'll tell you a secret. Right now Samara is in total puppy love over this boy she hopes will be at the dance tomorrow night. I mean, it's like the *perfect* opportunity for the rest of us to tease her and drive her crazy. And believe me, we'd love to, but guess who won't let us?"

"Heavenly?" Wes guessed.

"Right," I said. "She's really sensitive about things like that."

Just then Heavenly came down the stairs with a sleepy-looking Tyler in her arms. When she saw Wes, she smiled. "Hi, Wes, how are you?"

"F-Fine," Wes stammered. "And you?"

"Just great," Heavenly said cheerfully and went into the kitchen.

As soon as the kitchen door swung closed, I turned to Wes. "Now, come on, isn't she nice?"

Wes nodded.

"I can't swear to you that she'll want to work at the dance," I said. "But I *can* swear to you that if she can't, she'll be really nice about it."

Wes took a deep breath and let it out slowly. He stared at the closed kitchen door.

I started to get up. "Come on, big guy, let's give it a try and see what happens."

Chapter

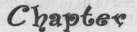

16

Wes finally agreed. He and I went into the kitchen together. Heavenly was making a salad for dinner. Tyler was on his hands and knees on the floor pretending he was a puppy.

"Woof!" he barked at the puppy, who cocked his head and gave him a puzzled look.

"Woof!" Tyler barked again.

The puppy put his tail between his legs and scurried away.

Now it was Tyler's turn to look puzzled. But as soon as he saw Wes he forgot about the puppy and waddled over.

"Wessy! Wessy!" he chirped happily and sat down on Wes's foot. Then he wrapped his pudgy arms and legs around Wes's ankle.

"Ride, Wessy! Ride!"

Before Wes could say anything to Heavenly, he

had to walk around the kitchen with Tyler on his foot. Each time he swung his leg Tyler held on and cheered with delight.

Of course, every time Wes stopped, Tyler would say "More, Wessy! More!" until Heavenly finally came over and made him get off our piano teacher's foot.

"That's enough, Tyler," Heavenly said firmly and led him away.

Without Tyler to give a ride to, Wes didn't seem to know what to do. He gave me a nervous look. I got the feeling he was about to run.

"You must be thirsty after all that teaching and walking, Wes," I said. "Wouldn't you like something to drink?"

"Uh . . ." Wes looked so uncomfortable that he didn't know what to say.

"Why don't you ask Heavenly what we've got," I suggested.

"Uh . . ." Wes even seemed to be having trouble with that. But Heavenly heard me and went over to the refrigerator.

"Iced tea, water, milk, orange juice, and ginger ale," she said.

"Uh, iced tea, please," Wes managed to croak.

Heavenly poured a glass and handed it to him.

"Th-thank you," he stammered.

"You're welcome." Heavenly turned back to the kitchen counter to finish the salad.

Wes gave me a nervous look. Without speaking, I moved my lips as if to say, "Go ahead, ask her."

Wes swallowed and looked at Heavenly.

"Uh . . ."

Heavenly looked up at him. "Yes?"

Wes blinked, then quickly shook his head. "Nothing."

Heavenly frowned, then looked back down. Wes gave me a helpless look.

Again I moved my lips, this time as if to say, "Go on, don't be afraid."

Wes pursed his lips with frustration as if his mind wanted to ask, but he couldn't quite get his mouth to cooperate. It was becoming obvious that if I waited for Wes to get up the nerve to speak, we'd be here for several more days.

"Heavenly," I said, "Wes wants to ask you a question."

Heavenly looked up. "What about?"

Wes started to open his mouth. This time no sound at all came out.

"About the dance," I said for him.

"What about it?" Heavenly asked.

"Wes is going to be the DJ," I said.

"Really?" Heavenly looked surprised.

"Yes," Wes managed to say.

"Have you ever DJ'd a dance before?" Heavenly asked.

"No," said Wes.

"Oh." Heavenly frowned.

"That's what he wants to talk to you about," I said.

"What?" said Heavenly. "About being a DJ?"

"No, dancing," I said.

"Dancing?" Heavenly repeated.

"Wes needs a dancer," I explained. "You know, someone to get everyone going."

"So?" said Heavenly.

"So he was hoping maybe you'd want to do it," I said.

"Me?" Heavenly frowned again.

"I told him you were a great dancer," I said.

Heavenly turned to Wes. "You want me to be your dancer?"

Wes nodded eagerly.

"He'll pay you, of course," I added.

Wes nodded again.

"Well . . ." Heavenly thought it over. "I could definitely use the money."

"Then you'll do it?" I asked hopefully. Wes's eyes went wide.

"I'll think about it," Heavenly said and went back to the salad.

Chapter

17

Wes's shoulders sagged with disappointment.

Just then the kitchen door swung open, and Robby stuck his head in. "Hey, Wes, isn't it time for my lesson?" he asked.

"Right." With his head hanging, Wes dragged his feet out of the kitchen.

I waited until the door swung shut. Then I turned to Heavenly. "What's with you?" I asked.

Heavenly looked up, surprised. "With me?"

"You hurt his feelings," I said.

"I did?" Heavenly looked bewildered.

"Didn't you see how much he wanted you to do it?" I asked.

Heavenly shook her head. "How could I see that? He hardly said a word."

"It's what he *didn't* say," I stressed.

"He didn't say anything," Heavenly said.

"That's the whole point!"

"I don't know what you're talking about," Heavenly said.

"Wes was too nervous to speak," I explained. "The more he wants something, the less he says. So when he really, *really* wants something, he can't say anything."

"Now, that makes perfect sense." Heavenly smirked.

"That's just the way he is," I said.

"Can you imagine what he must've been like in school?" Heavenly said. "The more he needed to use the bathroom, the less he could ask. I'm glad I didn't have to sit next to *him*."

"He's just very, very shy," I said.

"Very, very *strange* is more like it."

"Oh, come on, Heavenly," I pleaded. "Just go out there and tell him you'll do it. You'll really make him happy."

"I said I'd think about it," Heavenly replied firmly.

"Can't you even say which way you're leaning?" I asked.

"I'm leaning toward telling you that it's none of your business and stop being so pushy," Heavenly replied. "Now, why don't you sit down and finish your homework?"

"In a second," I said, and left the kitchen.

Out in the living room Wes was giving Robby his piano lesson. Even though he was the youngest member of our family who took lessons, Robby practiced the most and was the best piano player among us. That's why Wes always saved him for last.

Wes gave me a sad look.

"Don't give up," I said. "She didn't say she wouldn't do it. She just said she wanted to think about it."

"Think about what?" Robby asked.

I explained how Wes was DJ-ing the dance and needed a dancer, and how he hoped Heavenly would do it.

"Sounds cool," Robby said.

"She's not going to do it," Wes moped.

"How do you know?" Robby asked.

"When she said she'd think about it, she was just being polite," Wes said. "When a girl says she'll think about something, it means she's going to say no. She just wants to foam the runway first."

"Foam what runway?" Robby repeated. "What are you talking about?"

"It's what they do at airports when a plane is coming in for a crash landing," Wes said. "They foam the runway. It's supposed to help keep the plane from catching fire."

"But what's that got to do with Heavenly?" I asked.

"Pretend I'm the airplane," Wes said. "I'm about to crash and it's going to hurt. Heavenly's just being nice. She doesn't want to hurt my feelings."

"So she's foaming the runway," I added.

"I hate to say this, but I think you're both crazy," Robby said.

"You're probably right," Wes said wistfully.

"Don't give up," I said. "I'll work on Heavenly some more. There's still hope."

Chapter 18

That evening after dinner everyone helped clean up. Samara didn't say anything about the dance, but you could tell by the way she kept humming happily to herself that she was thinking about seeing Parker Marks.

Most nights while we cleaned the kitchen, Heavenly gave Tyler a bath. So when we finished, I went upstairs to the nursery to talk to her. Lots of laughter and barking were coming from the nursery. I went in, but no one was there. The door to the bathroom was open, and that's where all the noise was coming from.

I went in. Heavenly was on her knees beside the bathtub. Tyler and the puppy were both in the bathtub, covered with suds.

Woof! Woof! The puppy barked excitedly as Tyler blew small clumps of suds at him. The puppy kept snapping at the suds, but they'd just disappear in his mouth. And then he'd look confused, as if he couldn't figure out where the suds went. And that, of course, would make Tyler laugh.

No one noticed me. I was just about to say something when I noticed the earring in Heavenly's left ear. Actually, she had a lot of earrings in that ear, but they were mostly small hoops. But the earring I was interested in was the one in her earlobe. It was a rounded, bright red stone with a tiny black-and-white head and black spots. In fact, it was made to look just like a ladybug.

And that was the ear Heavenly always seemed to touch just before something strange happened.

I had another thought and quickly looked around. Sure enough, a bright red ladybug was crawling on the ceiling over us.

What was it about Heavenly and ladybugs? I wondered.

"Oh, hello!"

The sound of Heavenly's voice made me jump. She was still kneeling beside the bathtub, looking up over her shoulder at me.

"Hi," I said.

"What's up?" she asked.

"Saving water?" I asked back, nodding at Tyler and the puppy in the tub together.

Heavenly looked back down at Tyler and the puppy. "Saving energy is more like it. They both needed a bath, so why not?"

"I'm surprised you didn't throw Puff in there," I said, referring to our cat.

"The kitchen clean?" Heavenly asked.

"Spotless," I said.

Heavenly gave me a look as if she didn't believe me.

"Okay," I admitted. "Almost spotless."

"Homework all done?" she asked.

"Almost," I said.

"Why not finish it?"

"I will, in just a second," I said. "First I want to talk about Wes."

Heavenly gave me a weary look. "I think we've exhausted the subject, Kit."

"Not quite," I said. "You know he really wants you to work at the dance. I don't understand why you won't. It's not like he's asking you on a *date*. It's just a job. You'll make some money. You'll have fun and you'll be doing Wes a favor. What could be so bad about that?"

"It's difficult to explain, Kit," Heavenly said.

"Hey, I'm all ears," I replied.

Heavenly turned back to the tub and wrapped Tyler in a towel. Then she lifted him out and began to rub him down. Tyler giggled. The puppy put his wet paws against the bathtub wall and stood on his hind feet barking as if he wanted to get out, too.

"Just a minute, pup," Heavenly said.

"Does it have something to do with Shackelford and Litebody?" I asked.

A look of shock crossed Heavenly's face. "How—"

"How what?" I said.

"How . . . interesting that you should say that," Heavenly said.

"Why?"

"Did someone say something?" Heavenly asked.

"Maybe," I said.

"Well, that has nothing to do with this," Heavenly said as she lifted the puppy out of the tub and started to rub him down with the towel.

"But you know what I'm talking about?" I asked.

Heavenly nodded.

"What happened?" I asked.

"We'll talk about it another time," Heavenly said.

"Oh, come on," I argued. "That's what you always say. And then we never talk about it."

"All right," Heavenly said. "Just let me put Tyler to bed. Would you warm up some water? I feel like some tea."

I went down to the kitchen and put on the water. I have to admit I was feeling nervous and excited. For the past month Heavenly's background had been a mystery. Maybe now I would get some answers.

A little while later Heavenly came in and made herself a cup of tea. "I don't know who's cuter. That little boy or that little puppy," she said. "So, you found out about Shackelford and Litebody."

"Yes."

"May I ask how?"

"A friend of mine was looking through a book of old pictures of Soundview Manor," I explained.

Heavenly nodded. "And?"

"Your ancestors were the first settlers of Soundview Manor?" I said.

"Yes, I believe that's true," Heavenly said.

"Then what happened?" I asked.

Heavenly chuckled. "Have you got a few years for me to explain?"

"How about just the Shackelford and Litebody part?" I asked.

"Well, when the Litebodys first arrived here, they built homes and started several businesses," Heavenly said. "Soon other families moved to Soundview Manor. Some of them started their own businesses, and others went into my family's business."

"I know!" I said. "The Shackelfords went into a competing business!"

"No, the Shackelfords went into my family's business," Heavenly said.

"What business was that?" I asked.

"The sewing machine business," Heavenly said.

I was just about to ask more questions when the phone rang. It was Dad calling from Korea, and whenever he called from far away, he liked to talk to all the kids. By the time everyone had a chance to talk, it was getting late, and Heavenly said it was time to go to bed.

Chapter 19

The next day at lunch in school I told Darcy what I'd learned.

"She said her family, the Litebodys, started this business and the Shackelfords went to work for them," I said.

"Well, that explains the sign on that building," Darcy said. "But did you ask her what happened to her family?"

"I was just about to, and then Dad called from Korea," I said. "And by the time we were all finished talking to him, it was time to go to bed."

"So, ask her tonight," Darcy said.

"I will," I said, "but I can tell she's going to try to avoid it."

"Don't let her," Darcy said. "But this is just the kind of mystery I love, so I'm going to keep looking, too."

"Hello, ladies," Roy said as he placed his tray down on the table with us.

"Hi, Roy," Darcy said.

"So." Roy rubbed his hands together. "Ready for the dance tonight?"

Darcy frowned. "What are you talking about? Only the sixth graders are going."

"Kit didn't tell you?" Roy asked. "We're going, too."

"We're working the refreshment table," I explained.

"How romantic," Darcy said.

Roy's face actually turned red. "That's not why I asked Kit to do it!"

"She didn't say it was," I explained. "She was just making a joke."

"Oh. Okay, sorry."

Darcy gave me a wink. Romance was obviously a subject Roy was sensitive about. I guess we all knew that even though we were only supposed to be "working" together that evening, Roy would have other things on his mind.

"I wouldn't get too excited about this dance," Darcy said. "Guess who's in charge of the decorations?"

"Who?" I asked.

Darcy nodded her head toward the superpopular table, where Jessica "Have It All" Huffington held court each day. Jessica was blond and blue-eyed and the richest girl in school. As I explained before, she used to ignore me. But that had mysteriously changed after Heavenly got involved. Now Jessica and I were friendly, at least in school.

"Jessica?" I guessed.

Darcy nodded. "You're talking about a girl whose sense of style and taste would give half the wrestlers in the WWF nightmares."

"But it's a dance," I said. "How badly could she mess it up?"

Darcy smiled. "I guess you'll see, won't you?"

The rest of the day went slowly. I can't say I minded. I took the time to think about Roy. He really was a sweet boy, and it was still puzzling to me that I wasn't thrilled that he liked me. I mean, after all those months of wishing he'd like me, why was I suddenly so uncertain about him?

Maybe he was right about "sweet" boys. Maybe they were the ones girls just liked to talk to.

School ended for the day. I was going down the hall toward the front doors when I passed the gym. Remembering Darcy's prediction at lunch, I decided to take a peek inside and see what Jessica was up to.

I pulled open the gym doors and couldn't believe my eyes. Jessica and a bunch of her friends were indeed working on the decorations. They were standing on ladders, stringing crepe-paper streamers, blowing up balloons, and taping down tablecloths on the refreshment tables.

It really would have been nice.

If it wasn't all brown.

"Oh, hi, Kit!" Jessica came toward me with a big smile on her face. I still found it hard to believe how friendly she'd become since our little disagreement over Roy.

"Hi, Jess," I said.

"So what do you think?" she asked, sweeping her arms around as if showing off her handiwork.

"It's very, uh, earthy," I said, searching hard for a compliment.

"Exactly!" Jessica said. "I mean, you can't believe how hard it was to pick these colors. I thought, well, we couldn't use blue and white because those are Soundview's colors and it would upset Marwich. And we couldn't use orange and black for the same reason. And then I thought, well, it's a fall dance, and fall colors are all sort of neutrals and browns, and wouldn't that be perfect!"

"Perfect," I repeated, *if you wanted to call it the Mud Dance.*

"So I hear you're working at the refreshment table with Roy," Jessica said.

"Yes." I nodded.

Jessica grinned. "He's so sweet."

"Will you be there?" I asked.

"Definitely," Jessica said. She moved close and whispered, "I'm going to stand right by the door so I can hear everyone's reactions as they come in."

"That should be interesting," I said.

We said goodbye, and I left the gym. What would be interesting would be Samara's reaction to the decorations that night. I mean, her red dress and those brown colors. Talk about a clash!

On the way home the sky was a dome of dark gray with smaller, lighter clouds racing by beneath. The wind was whistling through the trees, and the branches were swaying and creaking.

When I let myself into the house, I found Samara waiting for me in the front hall. "Don't go anywhere," she said and then hurried into the kitchen.

A moment later she returned, tugging Heavenly by the wrist.

"Kit, could you be a dear and watch Tyler and the puppy while I take Samara out for a new pair of shoes?" Heavenly asked. "Tyler will be ready for a nap soon, and you can put the puppy in his crate."

"What's wrong with the shoes Samara has?" I asked.

"They're old," Samara said. "I couldn't possibly wear them to the dance tonight."

"I thought you just got them a few weeks ago," I said.

"I did, but I've already worn them twice," said Samara, who went past me and outside.

Heavenly was following her, but I stopped her. "You're not really going to get her a new pair of shoes."

"It's her first real dance," Heavenly replied. "It's her first real crush. This is a very big moment in a young woman's life. If a new pair of shoes will make her feel better, then why not?"

Heavenly and Samara left. I went into the kitchen and played with Tyler until he started to yawn and rub his eyes. I put the puppy in his crate and then took Tyler upstairs for his nap.

As soon as Tyler fell asleep, I went to the bathroom to take a shower and get ready for the dance. I was back in my room drying my hair and putting on makeup when I heard a knock on the door.

"Who is it?" I asked.

"Robby," came the answer. The door swung open, and my little brother stood in the doorway. "Ready?"

"For what?"

"We're going to hide Samara's dress, remember? It's the trap we're going to set to see if Heavenly's a Wiccan."

I hesitated. "I don't know, Robby."

Robby got a pained look on his face. "Don't tell me you're gonna chicken out."

"I'm not chickening out," I said. "I just think it's mean to hide Samara's dress."

"But she deserves it," Robby insisted.

"I'm not saying she doesn't," I replied. "I just wish there was some other way we could figure out if Heavenly's a Wiccan that wasn't so mean."

"But you know Heavenly's going to make a new dress appear," Robby said.

"No, I don't," I said.

"Believe me, Kit, she will," Robby said firmly.

"Will what?" It was Chance, standing in the hallway behind Robby.

"Nothing," I said.

Chance stepped past Robby and came into my room. "Hey, Kit, lookin' sharp."

"Stop teasing, Chance," I said, feeling my face get hot.

"I'm not teasing," Chance said. "What's the occasion?"

"Roy Chandler asked me to help him with the drink table at the dance tonight," I explained.

Chance made a face. "You're getting all dressed up for that geek?"

"He's *not* a geek and I'm *not* getting dressed up for him," I replied. "I'm just getting dressed for the dance. And anyway, what do you care?"

"Uh, excuse me, Chance," Robby interrupted, "but Kit and I have something to do, and if we don't do it soon, we're going to run out of time."

"Forget it, Robby," I said. "I'm not doing it."

"But you promised!" Robby whined.

"No, I didn't," I said.

"Yes, you did," Robby insisted. "We talked about it and you agreed. And agreeing is like promising, so you promised."

"The only thing I agreed to was that it would be

nice if someone knocked Samara off her high horse," I countered.

"Sounds good to me," said Chance.

"That's it!" Robby cried. "If you won't do it, Kit, I'll get Chance to do it."

"No," I said.

"Do what?" asked Chance.

Robby explained how he wanted to hide Samara's dress in order to force Heavenly to do magic.

"Magic?" Chance repeated with a frown.

"Heavenly's a Wiccan," Robby said. "It's like a sorceress. She can do magic."

"You mean, like tricks?" Chance asked.

"No, *real* magic," Robby said. "Like sorcery and stuff. Charms and spells."

Chance chuckled. "I think you've been playing too many video games, little dude."

"I'm serious," Robby said. "Ask Kit."

Chance gave me a funny look.

"I'm not really sure," I said. "I just think it might be possible."

"Are you for real?" Chance asked.

I reminded him of how Heavenly always managed to get into the house no matter how often we changed the code on the security system, and of the time the tabs on the soda cans kept breaking off and the doorknob came off in his hand.

"It just seems like ever since Heavenly got

here, some really odd things have happened," I concluded.

"Listen, Kit, Robby's ten," Chance said patiently. "He's still a kid. But you're fourteen, and you should know there's no such thing as magic."

"Believe me, that's what I always thought," I agreed. "But ever since Heavenly showed up, I've started to wonder."

"I'm starting to wonder, too," Chance said. "But not about Heavenly. About *you*."

"This is dumb," Robby complained. "I'm not going to argue with you guys. If you won't help me hide Samara's dress, I'll do it myself."

"No!" I said.

But Robby ignored me and started out of the room. I was just about to follow him when the phone rang.

"Chance, would you please get it while I stop Robby?" I begged.

Chance shook his head and smiled. "No way. It's probably your boyfriend."

"He's *not* my boyfriend!" I yelled.

The phone kept ringing. It was obvious that Chance wasn't going to answer it.

"Thanks a lot, Chance," I grumbled and ran down to the kitchen. I really didn't care if it was Roy. But it might have been Darcy or another of my friends. I grabbed the phone and answered it. "Hello?"

"Kit, it's Wes."

"Oh, hi, Wes."

"Is Heavenly there?"

"No, she went out. She should be home pretty soon. Why don't you try calling back in a little while?" I didn't mean to be rude, but I wanted to get back upstairs and stop Robby before he hid Sarama's dress.

"Wait!" Wes said. "Did she say anything about the dance?"

"Well, not exactly," I said.

"Did you ask her?" Wes asked.

I didn't want to tell him that Heavenly had avoided the question every time I'd put it to her. But I didn't want to make him feel bad, either. Mostly I wanted to get off the phone fast before Robby did something to Samara's dress. "Listen, Wes, I think she'll probably do it. Now, I don't want to be rude, but—"

"That's great!" Wes said. "I'll be right over!"

"But—"

Click! Before I could explain anything more, he hung up. I thought about calling him back, but then decided it was more important to stop Robby first.

I hung up the phone and ran out of the kitchen and up the stairs. Robby was just coming out of Samara's room with the red dress in his hands. I blocked his path.

"I'm sorry, Robby, but I really think this is a bad idea," I said.

"You're just chicken," Robby replied.

"I am not chicken," I said. "I just don't think we have to be this mean."

"It's not being mean," Robby insisted. "It's just proving a point. No matter what I do with this dress, Heavenly will just conjure up a new one."

"You don't know that for a fact," I said.

"Wanna bet?" Robby asked.

"There's no point in betting because there's no way we're going to find out."

"There sure is," Robby said. He started to go around me.

"Stop!" I yelled.

"No!" Robby kept going.

"Yes!" I grabbed Samara's dress.

"Let go!" Robby yelled.

"*You* let go!" I yelled back.

"No!"

The next thing I knew, we were in a tug-of-war.

"You're so immature!" I shouted.

"And you're so chicken!" Robby shouted back.

"I am not!" I yelled. "I just don't think it's—"

"*What are you doing?*" Samara screamed as she came up the stairs with a shoebox under her arm.

Riiiiiipppppppppppp!

The dress tore in two.

Chapter

I can't believe you!" With clenched fists Samara ranted and stomped around the kitchen. "I just can't believe you!"

Robby and I sat at the kitchen table with our chins on our hands. I watched a ladybug crawl up the side of a glass. The whir of the sewing machine filled the room as Heavenly worked feverishly to sew the dress back together. Heavenly had insisted that Robby and I sit at the kitchen table so she could "keep an eye" on us and make sure we didn't get into any more trouble.

Outside the wind was really howling. Rain and sleet pelted the kitchen windows. The storm Robby had talked about the day before had arrived.

"I mean, what's wrong with you two?" Samara screeched.

"Stuff a sock in it, Samara," Robby grumbled.

113

"Robby!" Heavenly said sharply. "I think your sister has every right to vent her anger. What you two did was terrible."

"It was an accident," I tried to explain for the six millionth time.

"How could it be an accident?" Samara demanded. "You were both trying to tear my dress apart. I saw it with my own eyes."

"That's not what we were doing," I said.

"Then what were you doing?" Heavenly asked as she fed the torn dress through the sewing machine.

Robby and I exchanged guilty looks. It wasn't like we could explain what led up to us tearing the dress in half. I didn't want to say that I was trying to stop Robby from hiding the dress. That would only make Robby look bad. In the meantime the sewing machine continued to whir.

From the front hall came the sound of the doorbell ringing.

Heavenly looked up from the sewing machine and frowned. "Who could that be?"

"I'll go see." Robby started to get up.

"You're not going anywhere," Heavenly said.

The kitchen door swung open, and Chance stuck his head in. "Wes is here."

Heavenly's eyebrows rose with surprise. "What's he doing here?"

"Oh, my gosh!" I jumped up.

"Who said you could go anywhere?" Heavenly asked.

"I'll be right back, I swear." Before Heavenly could stop me, I dashed past Chance and went out to the front hall. Wes was standing just inside the front door, wearing a yellow rain slicker and heavy boots. Rainwater dripped down the slicker and fell to the floor. Wes's face was red from the cold, wet wind.

"Boy, it's a real mess out there," he said. "Is Heavenly ready?"

"She's, uh, just doing some last-minute alterations on Samara's dress," I said.

"Well, all right." Wes checked his watch. "It's still a little early. I guess I can wait."

"That's very nice of you," I said. "Just stay here. I'll be back in a moment."

I hurried back into the kitchen. As I went in, Samara came out. She narrowed her eyes angrily at me.

"I know why you tried to ruin my dress," she whispered.

"You do?" I replied.

"You're just jealous because a handsome, famous male model likes me," she said.

I couldn't believe it. "Samara, how could he like you if he doesn't even *know* you?"

Samara's eyes went wide with fury. She threw her head up and marched upstairs, saying she was going to wash her hair and get ready for the dance. I went back into the kitchen.

"So, did Wes say what he wants?" Heavenly asked while she continued to work on the dress.

I had a feeling it would be a bad idea to just come right out and tell her that Wes thought she was going to help him at the dance. It would be better if I worked up to it gradually.

"Remember that time when we were all dancing?" I asked.

"What about it?" Heavenly answered. She was bent over the sewing machine, slowly feeding the torn dress through.

"You have to admit it was fun," I said.

"It was fun until we woke up Tyler and your parents came home and threw a fit," Heavenly said.

"True," I admitted. "But up till that point."

"And what's *your* point, Kit?" Heavenly asked without looking up from the sewing machine. It was obvious she was very upset about the torn dress.

"Well, just that we really haven't had a chance to dance like that since," I said.

"So?"

". . . a dress and fix it up," Robby said with a grin.

"Very funny," Heavenly grumbled.

"I just think it would be a lot of fun to go out dancing sometime," I said.

"Uh-huh." Heavenly nodded, but she seemed distracted.

Just then the doorbell rang again.

"I'll get it!" I cried, sensing that I wasn't making much progress with Heavenly.

"No, you won't," Heavenly ordered. "You'll stay right here and explain what Wes is doing here. Robby will see who's at the door now."

"Aye-aye, Captain!" Robby stood up and saluted, then headed out of the kitchen.

Meanwhile, Heavenly stopped sewing and leveled her gaze at me. "Okay, Kit, what's the story?"

It was time to get serious. I sat down at the table across from her. "Heavenly, Wes really wants you to dance tonight. It's not just that he wants you to. He *needs* you to. This is his first job as a DJ, and if it doesn't go well, it may also be his last."

"Kit, we've been over this a hundred times," Heavenly said. "He doesn't need me to make it go well."

"He does," I insisted. "You know what sixth graders are like. If someone doesn't drag them out on the dance floor and make them dance, they'll just stand around all night and stare at each other. It'll be a disaster."

"I still don't see why he needs me," Heavenly said.

"Because you're older and you're pretty and you're a good dancer," I tried to explain. "The sixth-grade boys will be dying to dance with you. And once you get the boys dancing, the girls will join in, and the dance will be a huge success!"

Just then the door swung open and Robby came back in.

"Who was it?" Heavenly asked.

"It's Roy Chandler," Robby said. "He's here to pick up Kit and take her to the dance." My brother turned to me with a funny smile on his face. "And he brought you something!"

I knew I had to go out and greet Roy, but I didn't want to leave Heavenly until she'd made up her mind.

"So?" I said.

". . . a button on a sleeve," Heavenly replied.

"Just promise me you won't decide," I begged. "I'll be right back."

Out in the front hall Roy was standing next to Wes. Roy's jacket was soaked and glistening with rainwater. His hair was all wet and plastered down on his head. In his hand was a bunch of long green stems. Some of the stems had a few green leaves on them. He held them toward me.

"I, er, brought these for you," he said.

"Stems?" I said with a frown.

"Well, they were flowers when I left my house," Roy explained. "But you won't believe how windy it is outside."

Outside the roar of the wind through the trees did seem to be growing louder.

Meanwhile, Wes glanced at his watch again. "Uh, excuse me for interrupting, but is Heavenly ready yet?"

"Sorry, Wes," I answered. "She'll still be a minute."

Just then all the lights in the house flickered and went dark for a second before flashing back on.

"Oh, darn!" came Heavenly's wail from the kitchen.

Chapter

21

We rushed into the kitchen to see what the matter was. One thing I knew about Heavenly was that she wasn't the kind of person who yelled out unless it was really serious. We found her sitting with her elbows on the kitchen table and her chin in her hands. The corners of her mouth were turned down in a big frown and she almost looked like she was going to cry. In front of her, Samara's dress was jammed into the sewing machine. It looked like a big red bird's nest with lots of red threads sticking out in all directions.

"What happened?" Robby asked.

"I guess I was working too fast," she moped. "When the electricity flickered, it all jammed. Look at it! It doesn't even look like a dress anymore. I don't know what I'm going to do now."

"And just wait until Samara sees it," Robby said, giving me a knowing look.

I knew what he was thinking. If ever there was a time when Heavenly needed to use some magic, it was probably now.

"I know what," I said. "Let's all go back out into the front hall and leave Heavenly alone. I bet if she has some time by herself she can straighten this whole thing out."

"I don't see how leaving her alone is going to help," Wes said.

"I just think that if Heavenly's left alone and puts her mind to it, she can do it," I said.

Heavenly gave me the funniest look. As if she knew exactly why I'd suggested that. But before she could answer, Wes kneeled down beside the sewing machine and started to study the bird's nest dress.

"You might be right, Kit," he said. "But I think I can fix this and save her a lot of time."

"How?" asked Robby. "What do you know about sewing machines?"

"Plenty, my young friend," Wes replied as he started to pull off his wet rain slicker. "It just so happens that when my great-grandfather Horace Shackelford started the Shackelford Corporation, the first product he ever made was the Shackelford Silent Sewer. For years it was the premiere sewing machine in the world."

What Wes couldn't see was the expression on

Heavenly's face when he said that his great-grandfather started the Shackelford Corporation. Believe me, if looks could kill . . . One look at her and I gave up all hope of getting her to the dance that night.

"What about semiconductors?" Robby asked.

"I know this'll come as a shock to you, Robby," Wes said with a smile, "but back in the 1800s there were no computers. In fact, there was hardly any electricity. You ran the Shackelford Silent Sewer by rocking a foot peddle under the machine. My family didn't get into the computer business until the 1980s."

Suddenly I had an idea. "So you're saying your great-grandfather started the sewing machine company all by himself?"

"That's right," Wes said as he started to take apart the sewing machine.

"Was there ever a time when it wasn't called the Shackelford Corporation?" I asked.

Wes looked up with a scowl. "What do you mean?"

"Wasn't there a time when it was called Shackelford and Litebody?" I asked.

Wes frowned. "No, not to my knowledge. I mean, everyone knows the Litebodys were the first family to settle here in Soundview, but, um, I actually don't know what business they were in."

"Can I speak to you for a moment in the hall?"

I said to Heavenly. "While Wes tries to untangle the sewing machine?"

Heavenly rolled her eyes toward the ceiling. "If you insist."

We went out into the hall.

"Look, Heavenly," I said. "It's pretty obvious that if something happened between the Litebodys and the Shackelfords way back when, he doesn't know about it. I mean, I don't see how you can blame him for something he had nothing to do with."

"How do you know he isn't lying?" Heavenly asked.

"I'll tell you how I know," I said. "If Wes was lying, he'd be nervous. And if he was nervous, he wouldn't be able to speak. You know that."

"Why do you care so much?" Heavenly asked.

"Simple," I said. "Wes Shackelford is a really nice guy. And he likes you. He's not asking you to marry him, Heavenly. He's just asking if you'd help him out with his first job as a DJ. If you say yes, it doesn't mean you're in love with him. It just means you're a nice person and you're willing to do him a favor."

Heavenly let out a big sigh. "All right, Kit. If it means that much to you, I'll think about it."

"That's what you always say," I said.

"No." She shook her head. "I mean, I'll *really* think about it."

Heavenly stood perfectly still for a moment. I

wondered if she was thinking about it. But then she said, "Tyler's up."

"How do you know?" I asked. With all the stormy weather outside, I hadn't heard anything from upstairs.

"I just know," Heavenly said and hurried upstairs.

I went back into the kitchen. Wes had rolled up his sleeves and was still bent over the sewing machine.

A few moments later Heavenly came in with a sleepy-looking Tyler in her arms.

"Wessy!" Tyler cried and started to wiggle out of Heavenly's arms. "Ride, Wessy!"

"Sorry, little guy, I can't right now," Wes said.

Tyler stuck his lower lip out in a pout, but he seemed to understand. Meanwhile, Heavenly leaned over Wes's shoulder while he worked.

"You really think you can fix it?" she asked.

"I can definitely give it a try," Wes replied. "But I'll need some tools. A pair of pliers and the smallest screwdriver you can find."

"I'll go get them," Robby said.

Meanwhile, Wes continued to take the sewing machine apart. Heavenly sat down beside him and watched curiously while she held Tyler on her knee. I had a feeling I knew what she was thinking. This was a totally different person than the shy, stammering piano teacher who didn't seem to be able to string together two words when he was around her.

"Are you sure you know what you're doing, Wes?" she asked. "Just because your family used to make sewing machines doesn't mean you know how to fix them."

"I know what you're saying, Heavenly," Wes replied as he worked. "But I was one of those kids who was always taking things apart and putting them back together. I guess my family is pretty disappointed in me because I have no interest in going into the family business. All I like to do is fix things and play music."

"Really?" Heavenly said.

"Oh, yeah," Wes said. "Right now, I'm a major disappointment to the family. Mostly because I'm the only heir. If I don't take over the Shackelford Semiconductor Company, they'll probably have to sell it."

"They must be putting terrible pressure on you," Heavenly said.

Wes looked up at her and their eyes met. Wes blinked with astonishment as if he'd forgotten who he'd been talking to. His mouth opened, but no words came out.

Heavenly looked worried. "Are you okay?"

"Uh . . ." Wes began to stammer. "Okay? Uh . . ."

The kitchen door opened, and Robby came back in with a toolbox. "Here you go," he said.

"Right." Wes turned away from Heavenly and opened the toolbox. He took out a small screwdriver and a pair of pliers and got to work, opening the inside of the sewing machine. "Okay," he mumbled to himself. "I think I see the problem."

The rest of us huddled around, watching as he tinkered with the insides of the sewing machine like a surgeon. I felt a finger tap me on the shoulder. Swiveling around, I found Roy.

"Listen, Kit, we really should get over to the dance," he said. "There's a lot of setting up to do."

He was right. But there was one thing I had to do before I could go.

Chapter

22

Heavenly was still watching Wes work on the sewing machine. The look on her face was one of wonder and appreciation.

I caught her attention. "Think I could talk to you out in the hall again?"

Heavenly nodded. She put Tyler in his high chair and followed me out into the front hall. The rain and sleet were still pelting the windows, and the wind was howling. From outside came the sounds of tree branches creaking and cracking.

"So?" I said in a low voice.

". . . a button on a sleeve?" Heavenly replied.

"Be serious," I said. "You know what I'm talking about."

Heavenly nodded. "He's not what I expected."

"What do you mean?" I asked.

"Well, you know, for a *Shackelford*," she said.

"How do you know what a Shackelford is supposed to be like?" I asked.

"It's a long story."

"The same long story you were going to tell me last night before Dad called from Korea?" I asked.

"Uh-huh."

"I'm still all ears," I said.

But she shook her head. "Not now." She glanced back at the kitchen door.

"I think Wes has been nothing but really nice," I said. "Helping to fix the sewing machine and everything."

Heavenly nodded.

"The *least* you could do is help him out with the dance," I said.

"Yes, I know." Heavenly took a deep breath and let it out slowly. "I just *wish* he weren't a Shackelford."

"Why?" I asked.

Heavenly gave me a helpless look.

"It's a long story?" I guessed.

"Right."

The kitchen door opened, and Roy stuck his soggy head out. "He fixed it!"

"Great!" Heavenly and I hurried back into the kitchen.

Wes was putting the sewing machine back together. "There she is, good as new."

"You're a doll." Heavenly gave him a quick kiss on the cheek, then sat down at the sewing machine and went back to work on Samara's dress. Wes stood with his mouth hanging open and his hand on the spot on his cheek where Heavenly had kissed him.

"You okay?" I asked, worried he might faint.

"Uh . . . I . . . th-think . . . s-s-so," Wes stammered.

"Great!" Roy clapped his hands together. "Come on, Kit, we'd better get going."

"Just give me a second," I said, and hurried back up the stairs and into my room.

I sat down at my makeup table. I'd planned to wear my hair loose to the dance, but because of the wind and rain, I decided it might be better to put it into a braided ponytail. I could always take it out when I got to the dance.

I was in the middle of braiding my hair when I heard a knock on the door.

"Who is it?" I called.

"Take a Chance?" my stepbrother called from the other side of the door. The doorknob turned slightly and then stopped because it was locked.

"What do you want?" I called back.

"I have important news," he said. "Can I come in?"

"Oh, okay." I went to the door and let him in, then went back to my makeup table. Chance sat down on my bed behind me. I could see him in my mirror.

"Your boyfriend's here," he said.

"I know," I said.

"*Ah-ha!*" Chance jumped to his feet and shouted loud enough to make me drop my mascara stick. "Then you admit it!"

I swiveled around in my chair to face him. "What?"

"That he's your boyfriend," Chance said.

"He's *not* my boyfriend!"

"You just said he was," Chance said.

I stared at him for a moment. "Chance, can I tell you something?"

Chance sat down on my bed again. "What?"

I started to count on my fingers. "One, you're sixteen, but you're acting like you're eight. Two, Roy Chandler is *not, and never has been*, my boyfriend. Three, even if Roy Chandler *was* my boyfriend, it's none of your business."

Chance just sat there and watched me with his piercing blue eyes. I felt a chill and knew it wasn't from the wind outside. It was from the fact that even though he was my stepbrother and was acting like a jerk, he was *still* probably the best-looking boy in Soundview Manor.

"Why are you looking at me like that?" I finally asked, feeling uncomfortable under his gaze.

"Your hair looked nice before," he said. "How come you're pulling it back?"

"If I don't pull it back, it'll get all messed up by the wind."

A moment passed while he just sat there and

looked at me again. I turned back to the mirror and saw that the braid had fallen out while I was talking to him. "Oh, darn!"

"What's wrong?" he asked.

"My braid fell out. It's such a pain."

"I bet it would be easier if someone did it for you," Chance said, getting up.

The next thing I knew, Chance was standing behind me, braiding my hair!

"What do you know about braiding hair?" I asked, looking at his reflection in the mirror.

"You'd be surprised," he said, without looking up.

"That's for sure," I said. "This isn't a trick, is it? You're not tying it into knots, are you?"

With a devilish smile Chance looked up and caught my eye in the mirror. "What do you think I am? An eight-year-old?"

"Very funny."

Chance continued to braid my hair. I have to admit that it felt very odd to have his hands in my hair. But I tried not to think of it because, after all, he was my stepbrother and he was only braiding my hair.

Chapter

23

"Kit?" The sound of Roy's voice calling from downstairs shook me out of the spell.

"There's Romeo," Chance chuckled. "His timing's good. I just finished."

I felt him let go of my hair. But he didn't move away. Instead, he stood behind me, looking at me in the mirror as I gazed back.

What is he thinking? I wondered.

For that matter, what was I thinking?

"Hey, Kit!" Roy called again. "You up there?"

"You'd better go," Chance said. "You don't want to keep the king of the refreshment table waiting."

"Don't make fun of him," I said. "He happens to be a very sweet guy."

"I'm sure he is," Chance said.

"Besides," I said, "I promised him I'd help tonight."

"Uh-huh." Chance nodded, and I wondered who I was trying to convince that I really had to go. Him or me? I wasn't seriously thinking of ditching Roy to hang around the house all evening with Chance . . .

Was I?

I shook the idea out of my head. I must have been out of my mind. Chance was my stepbrother. And that was a total, definite no-no. Besides, he wasn't my type. He was never serious about anything. He broke girls' hearts without even trying!

"Hey, Kit, come on!" Roy called from downstairs. "We have to get going!"

Up in my room Chance gave me a funny look. "Something wrong?"

Yes! I thought. Something was very wrong. I'd had a crush on Roy for a long time. I'd always thought he'd be the perfect boy for me. He was nice, and reliable, and not the sort of boy you'd have to worry about some other girl trying to steal from you.

And now what I'd always imagined was coming true. Roy seemed to be crazy about me. But instead of being thrilled, I was completely confused.

I heard footsteps coming up the stairs and down the hall. Then a polite knock on my door.

"Kit?" Roy called from outside.

"I'm coming," I called and slid my chair back.

Chance and I shared one last look. He had a teasing smile on his face. "Impatient young man, isn't he?" he whispered with a smile and a wink.

"Hush!" I hissed, and went to the door. I pulled it open.

Roy stood outside in the hall with a funny expression on his face. "Everything okay?" he asked, looking past me and into my room.

I turned. Chance was nowhere to be seen! He must have been hiding behind the bed.

"Oh, yes," I said, stepping out of the room and pulling the door closed behind me. "I was just getting ready."

We went down the hall toward the stairs. Once again I could hear the roar of the wind and the rain and sleet hitting the windows. It seemed odd that a few minutes before, with Chance, I'd been completely unaware of the storm.

"Looks pretty bad outside," Roy said.

"Good thing it's not an outdoor dance," I quipped.

"What?" Roy scowled, then grinned. "Oh, yeah. That's a good one, Kit."

We went downstairs and into the kitchen. I couldn't believe my eyes. Samara was standing on a stool, wearing her red dress, while Heavenly did final alterations. Only Samara wasn't actually touching the stool. She was *floating* about four inches above it!

I quickly looked around to see if anyone else had noticed.

Wes was packing up the sewing machine. Tyler was sitting in his high chair eating cut-up pieces of banana. Robby's face was buried in a *Mad* magazine. The puppy was on the floor, licking his paw.

No one appeared to be aware that Samara was floating. Not even Samara!

"Ahem!" I cleared my throat loudly.

Thump! Samara landed on the stool and looked startled.

"Finished?" I asked Heavenly.

"Yes," she answered.

"It looks great," Wes said.

"It looks brand new," I said, giving Robby a curious look.

Robby shrugged. "Heavenly worked really hard on it."

I could tell he was disappointed that he hadn't proved Heavenly was a Wiccan. If only he'd looked up from his comic book earlier.

"Well, I guess it's time to go to the dance," Wes said, giving Heavenly a curious look.

And just then the lights went out.

Chapter

24

The kitchen was dark. For a second no one said a word. We were all waiting to see if the lights were going to come back on.

They didn't. Both the puppy and Tyler began to whimper.

"Dark," Tyler said with a frightened tremble in his voice.

"You're right, Mr. Wiggler," Heavenly said and scooped him up into her arms. Outside the wind continued to roar.

"Scared," Tyler whimpered.

"There's nothing to be scared of," Heavenly assured him. "It may be dark, but you're still in your nice, strong, warm house."

"Warm for now," I said, knowing from past experience that when the lights went out, so did the furnace that heated the house.

The kitchen door swung open, and Chance came in with a flashlight. "And so the fun begins," he announced with a chuckle, sweeping the bright beam of light around the kitchen until it stopped on the cabinet above the refrigerator. "Time to check the candle supply."

Fortunately, we had lots of candles. A few minutes later the kitchen glowed with the light of a dozen candles clustered on the kitchen table.

"Pretty," Tyler chirped, reaching toward them.

"Pretty, but hot," Heavenly warned. "Don't touch or it'll hurt."

"Hot, hurt," Tyler repeated, pulling his hand back.

"Now what?" Robby asked.

"Good question," I said. Even though we were inside, the wind outside was blowing so hard that drafts managed to get into the house and make the candle flames flicker and slant. I could already begin to feel a difference in the air. It was getting colder.

"Does anyone besides me feel it starting to get cooler in here?" I asked.

"I feel it," Chance said.

"Let's go to the dance," Samara said.

"There's not going to be a dance, dummy," Robby said. "The electricity's out."

"You don't know that," Samara said. "Just because it's out around here doesn't mean it's out at the school."

"Call the electric company," Wes suggested.

"Good idea." Robby went to the phone.

"If the electricity is out, the phone won't work," Samara said.

"It probably will," said Roy. "The phone company uses its own supply of electricity."

We waited while Robby called the electric company.

"Why did the peanut dial nine-one-one?" he asked while he dialed.

"Why?" asked Heavenly.

"Because he was assaulted," Robby said.

Everyone smiled. Robby listened on the phone for a few moments, then hung up. "All I got was a tape recording. There are scattered outages everywhere, and they've got crews out working as fast as they can."

"So there could still be a dance," Samara said hopefully.

"I guess the only way to really know is to go over to the school and see," said Wes.

Another cold draft of air wafted through the kitchen. I felt a chill.

"You know, I have a feeling we all ought to go," I said. "I mean, if there's electricity there, it'll be a lot better than staying here."

"What'll Chance and I do at the dance?" Robby asked.

"Well, I bet you could help Wes be the DJ," I said. "And Chance could watch Tyler while Heavenly dances."

I have to admit that a lot of that suggestion was wishful thinking on my part. I doubted Chance would want to watch Tyler, so I was surprised when he agreed.

"Are you sure you want to watch Tyler?" Heavenly asked him.

"Hey, it's better than hanging around here in the cold and dark," Chance answered, but then he gave me the strangest look, and I suddenly wondered if there wasn't another reason he wanted to come.

"Wait a minute," Samara said. "What about the puppy?"

"We'll have to leave him," I said. "I don't think the cold would bother him."

"Being left alone in the dark might," said Robby.

"Then we'll leave the candles burning," Samara said.

"No," said Heavenly. "You can't leave candles burning in an empty house. It's not safe."

"But no one's going to knock them over," Robby said.

"You never know," said Heavenly. "Puff might climb up on the table and knock one over, or one might just fall."

"I'd hate to leave the puppy alone in the dark," Samara said.

"Wow, this I can't believe," said Robby. "I didn't think anything would stop you from going to the dance."

"He's just a poor defenseless little thing," Samara said.

"Maybe we can take him," said Wes.

"They won't let you take him inside," Chance said. "And given the choice between sitting in the cold dark van and the cold dark house, I'd take the house."

"Wait a minute," Roy said. "I've got an idea! Do you guys have a big flat pan?"

"Like a cookie sheet?" Heavenly asked.

"No," said Roy. "It has to have sides."

"Let me see," said Heavenly.

"Heck of a time to bake a cake," Chance said.

"No, watch," said Roy.

Heavenly found a big flat pan with sides. Using the wax from the candles, Roy stuck a bunch of candles right in the middle of the pan. Then he poured about an inch of water in.

"See?" he said as he relit the candles, "now even if one falls, it's just going to fall into water."

"Very impressive invention," Wes said.

"You could call it the Chandler Self-Dousing Water Candle," said Robby.

"Kit said you were an inventor," said Heavenly. "I guess she wasn't kidding."

Roy beamed proudly. I noticed that Chance stood outside the circle of candlelight with a frown on his face. Could he possibly be jealous?

Chapter

25

A little while later we all stood in the front hall getting bundled up in raincoats and hoods. The puppy had followed us and started to yip excitedly.

"He thinks he's coming with us," I said.

"He has to stay in his crate," said Samara. "Otherwise he could get hurt while we're gone."

She picked him up and carried him back into the kitchen. Meanwhile, Heavenly took an umbrella out of the closet.

"Who do you think you are, Mary Poppins?" said Robby. "Forget the umbrella. It'll get ripped to shreds in that wind."

Heavenly put the umbrella back in the closet. Samara came back from the kitchen. Behind her we could hear the puppy yelping and crying. It wasn't because of the storm. He never wanted to be left alone.

"I hate it when he cries," she said. "Come on, let's go before I change my mind."

"I didn't think anything could change your mind about going to this dance," Robby said. "At least, not anything human."

Samara made a face. "You think you're so funny."

"Everyone ready?" Chance asked.

"Ready as we'll ever be," I answered.

"Here goes!" Chance pulled open the front door. A blast of cold wet air, freezing rain, and snow rushed in, nearly driving us backward.

"Brrrrr!" In no time we were all tucking our collars tight and complaining. We tromped out through the rain and slush toward Wes's van. The wind was so strong the rain was blowing sideways, and we had to hold our hats and lean forward in order not to get blown backward. In the dark we could see the big trees swaying back and forth and hear their leaves rustling angrily.

"Gee, what a miserable night!" Roy complained as we climbed into Wes's van.

"Why are we doing this?" asked Robby. A big cloud of white vapor came out with his breath.

"Oh, come on," said Heavenly as she strapped Tyler into his car seat. "We're in the van. At least we're not out in the rain. Let's have an adventure."

I'm not sure exactly how it happened, but somehow I wound up sitting with Roy on one side of me and Chance on the other. It might have been cold in the van, but it was somehow cozy, too. Wes turned the key, and the van rumbled to life. The windshield wipers started to swish back and forth. I turned to my right and saw a ladybug crawling across the window.

What in the world was it doing out on a night like this?

Crash! Out of nowhere a huge branch smashed to the ground beside us.

"Wow, let's get out of here!" Wes gasped. He turned around in his seat and quickly started to back the van down the driveway.

Things weren't much better out on Soundview Avenue. All the streetlights and house lights were out, and broken tree branches were lying all over the street. Wes drove slowly, carefully going around them.

"I hate to say it," Robby said. "But I don't see a light on anywhere. There's not going to be any electricity at school."

"We might as well go see," said Samara. "Like Heavenly said, we're in the van anyway."

Suddenly Wes jammed on the brakes.

"What's wrong?" Samara asked from the back.

"Have a look," said Heavenly from the front seat.

We all leaned forward and peered through the windshield. A tree trunk lay across the road in front of us.

"Think you could drive over it?" Heavenly asked Wes.

Wes stared at the tree trunk and shook his head. "It looks a little too big. I'm afraid I might damage the underside of the van."

"I say we go out and try to move it," said Chance.

"With our bare hands?" Roy asked.

"What's wrong?" Chance asked. "Afraid you'll get them dirty?"

"No," Roy replied. "I just think there must be a better way."

"Like what?" Chance challenged.

"Like . . . like using the van to move it!" Roy suddenly said.

"Hey, that's a good idea!" Wes agreed.

"Well, how're you going to do that?" Chance asked. You could see that he was upset that once again Roy had come up with a better idea.

"I think there's a rope in the back," Wes said. "We'll tie it around the tree and drag it out of the way."

"I say we just pick it up and move it," Chance muttered.

"No," Wes said. "Roy's idea is better. Come on, guys, let's go."

Wes and Roy started to get out of the van, but Chance just sat there with his arms crossed.

"Aren't you going to help?" Wes asked.

Chance shook his head stubbornly.

Wes went around to the back of the van and opened the doors. The cold wet wind whipped through the van as he got out the rope and then slammed the doors closed.

With the engine still running and the windshield wipers still swishing back and forth, we watched silently as Wes and Roy fought through the wind to the fallen tree trunk. Wes handed Roy the rope and then bent down and put his hands around the trunk.

"He's going to try to lift it," I said. "Then Roy will slide the rope underneath."

We watched as Wes tried to pull up on the log. We could see him straining and Roy poised with the rope, but the tree trunk wouldn't budge. Wes let go. He and Roy looked back at the van.

Heavenly swiveled around in the front seat. "They can't do it, Chance. They need your help."

"I told them it was a dumb idea," Chance grumbled.

"Chance, if they can't lift it to get the rope around it, they never would have been able to move it by hand, either," I pointed out.

Chance frowned, then pushed open the door and got out.

"What was that all about?" Robby asked as we watched Chance join Wes and Roy by the fallen tree.

"I think you'd better ask Kit," Heavenly said.

Robby gave me a puzzled look.

"I don't know what she's talking about," I said.

Outside we watched Wes and Chance bend down and strain to lift the tree just enough for Roy to get the rope under and around it. They tied a knot in the rope and then tied the other end to the front of the van.

"I sure hope this works," Wes said as he and the boys climbed back into the van. They were all breathing hard. Cold rainwater and melted snow dripped from their jackets.

"Hey, watch it!" Samara fumed as Roy climbed past her. "You want to get my dress all wet?"

"Is that how you thank someone?" Chance asked. "If it wasn't for what he just did, you wouldn't be going to the dance, period."

"I'm not saying I'm not thankful," Samara snapped. "I'm just saying he could be a little more careful."

Meanwhile, Wes put the van into gear. "Hold on, everyone."

He started to back the van up. The rope between the van and the tree went tight. In the headlights we watched it twist and grow thin and taut.

The log didn't budge.

"Rope might not be strong enough," Wes muttered.

"It'll work," said Chance.

In the darkness of the van I gave him a surprised look. "I thought you said your way would have been better."

"It would have," he answered with a smile. "But that doesn't mean this way's totally bogus."

The van kept backing up. The rope grew tighter and tighter . . .

Suddenly the tree began to move.

"All right!" Robby yelled.

Everyone let out whoops and cheers as Wes backed up the van, dragging the tree until it was parallel to the road.

Wes stopped the van and jumped out again, this time to untie the tree. A moment later he climbed back into the van. "Okay, everyone, let's just hope that's the last tree we encounter."

Samara crossed her fingers and shut her eyes. "Oh, please let it be the last tree. *Please!*"

I watched as Heavenly twisted around in the front seat and looked at her. She reached up and rubbed her left ear. I'd seen her do that before. Usually just before something "magical" happened.

The van started down the rainy windy dark road again. We passed more broken branches and limbs. Old dead brown leaves swirled and sailed through the air. Wes slowed down as a wind-blown garbage can rolled across the street in front of us. All the houses we passed were dark.

"This is weird," Robby said.

"I hate to say it, but we're getting pretty close

to school, and there are still no lights," Chance said.

"Don't say it!" Samara covered her face with her hands as if she couldn't bear to watch.

The school was only a few blocks away now. With all the lights out everywhere, it was difficult to tell just *how* close or far we were. But suddenly I realized we'd turned into the high school parking lot. The high school gym should have been directly in front of us. And on the night of a dance, it should have been brightly lit.

But all we saw was darkness.

Chapter

26

Bad news, Samara," Robby said solemnly.

"No, no, don't tell me." Samara still had her hands over her eyes.

"I'm afraid so, kid," Chance added.

"Oh, no!" Samara started to cry. In the front seat Wes gave Heavenly a questioning look as if asking what we could do. Heavenly shrugged.

Samara just kept bawling. Robby, Chance, and I shared pitiful looks. No matter how much we sometimes hated her, she was still our sister, and it hurt to see her so miserable.

"Well, I hate to say it, but there's no point in staying here," Wes said and started to turn the van around. Samara was still sobbing. For some reason, everyone turned around to look at the gym one last time. I guess we were all hoping a miracle might happen and the lights would go on.

149

A miracle . . .

I don't know why, but just at that second I turned toward the front.

Just in time to see Heavenly touching her left ear.

"Oh, wow!" Robby suddenly shouted.

"Stop the van!" yelled Chance.

I swiveled around again and looked out the back of the van.

The gym lights were on!

"Samara, look!" Wes said.

"No." Samara sobbed and kept her hands over her eyes. "This is the end. My life is ruined!"

"The lights are on, silly," I said.

"On?" Samara gasped as she lowered her hands from her face. "How?"

I looked at Heavenly, but she turned away.

"Who cares how?" said Wes. "Let's go!"

Wes pulled the van up close to the outside gym doors. The wind was still howling, and the rain was still coming sideways.

"Oh, no!" Samara cried, staring at her hands.

"Now what's wrong?" Robby asked.

"My makeup's smeared!" Samara buried her face in her hands again.

Robby rolled his eyes in disbelief. "That settles it. I just realized I'm the luckiest person in the world."

"Why?" Chance asked.

"Because I'm not a girl," Robby said.

"Chance, take Tyler," Heavenly said. "I'll help Samara with her makeup."

Meanwhile, Wes got out of the van and pulled open the back doors. We helped him take out his DJ equipment and carry it through the rain inside.

As we walked toward the gym, Robby and Roy went ahead of me.

"Oh, wow!" I heard Robby say as he stepped into the gym.

"Amazing!" agreed Roy.

It was hard to believe that they could be that excited about the decorations for what I was calling the Mud Dance.

But then I got into the gym and saw that it was amazing.

Truly amazing!

The whole gym was decorated like something out of a fairy tale, with huge black and gold and silver balloons, and long shimmering silver streamers.

There wasn't a speck of brown anywhere!

Chapter

27

I've been to dances before, but I've never seen anything like this," Roy said, amazed. "Where did all these decorations come from?"

"Good question," I said, glancing back through the open doors at the van. Heavenly was still inside it helping Samara with her makeup.

"They must've done it after school," said Chance.

Chance, being a guy, obviously didn't have a clue about how much work had to have gone into decorating the gym like that. It would have taken a dozen people a week to do it. And besides, I'd been in the gym that afternoon, and it hadn't been this color at all!

Roy looked at his watch. "The dance is going to begin in twenty minutes, everyone. We'd better get set up. Come on, Kit."

He grabbed my wrist and led me over to the refreshment table. We put out cups and pulled bottles of soda out of coolers of ice. Meanwhile Wes, Robby, and Heavenly set up the DJ equipment, and Chance and Tyler chased each other in a circle on the gym floor.

The gym doors swung open again. I expected to see Samara and Heavenly come in, but it was Jessica. She stopped just inside the doors and stared around with a shocked expression on her face. She even blinked and rubbed her eyes and looked again.

I turned to Roy. "Be back in a second."

"Don't be too long," Roy said. "People are going to start showing up any time now."

I hurried across the gym to Jessica. "Guess you changed your mind about the decorations, huh?"

Jessica looked like she was in a daze. "What?"

"The last time I saw you, you were decorating the gym in browns," I reminded her.

Jessica nodded slowly.

"You changed your mind, right?" I said.

Jessica turned to me. It seemed to take a while for her to focus. "Kit, I *did* decorate the gym in browns. I have no idea how this happened."

Just as I thought!

"Well," I said with a smile. "I think you did a beautiful job."

"But I . . . didn't do it," Jessica stammered.

"You must have," I said. "After all, you were in charge of the decorations."

Jessica gave me a suspicious look. "Why do I think you know what's going on here?"

"Listen, I'll be honest with you," I said. "I'm really not sure. But until I find out, you could do me a big favor by taking full credit for this fabulous job of decorating."

Jessica's suspicious look turned to a puzzled one, and then ended in a smile. "I will be *delighted* to take credit for this. I mean, compared to brown? What was I thinking?"

What, indeed? I thought with a smile and headed back to the refreshment table.

It wasn't long before the gym doors opened and kids began to stream in, oohing and ahhing at the sight of the fabulous decorations.

It was easy to tell the Marwich kids. They were the ones who hesitated and looked around as if they expected to be bombarded with water balloons. But once they saw that it was a real dance and not some kind of trick, they started to get into it.

Wes began to spin discs, and the gym filled with heavy thumping music. Someone turned the lights down and trained a spotlight on a huge mirrored ball hanging from the ceiling. The gym filled with sparkling, swirling lights.

Standing next to me at the refreshment table, Roy looked around with an awestruck expression on his face.

"Wow!" he said. "This is really amazing. I mean, first the gym lights go on and now this."

"You might say it's almost magical," I quipped.

"For sure!" said Roy. "Now, if only they'd start dancing."

He was right. The gym may have been beautiful, but it was just like every sixth grade dance I'd ever been to. The boys were standing around in groups looking at the girls, who stood around in groups and looked back. Except for Chance, who was on his knees pretending to dance with Tyler, the whole middle of the gym was empty.

Suddenly something red streaked toward me.

"He's here!" Samara gasped as she skidded to a stop in front of the refreshment table. Over her shoulder I saw Parker Marks standing with a group of Marwich guys, talking.

"Go ask him to dance," I said.

"Are you crazy!" Samara asked. "Never!"

"Why?" I teased. "I thought it was okay to call guys and ask them to dance."

"No way," said Samara.

"Then how are you going to get him to notice you?" Roy asked.

Samara pursed her lips and looked around. Suddenly a smile appeared on her lips. "See ya!"

She took off toward the stage, where Wes had set up his DJ equipment. Robby was standing behind the equipment with Wes. Suddenly Heavenly stepped onto the dance floor in front of the stage, wearing black tights and a black tank top with a loose white shirt over it. When she'd first come to our house, I'd guessed that she was about twenty-five. But tonight she looked younger. Samara ran to the stage and whispered something into Heavenly's ear.

"What's she up to?" Roy wondered out loud.

"She's up to being Samara," I said.

"What does that mean?" Roy asked.

"Being Samara means doing whatever it takes to get whatever she wants," I explained.

We watched as my stepsister and Heavenly left the stage together. Samara wandered off toward a crowd of her friends while Heavenly headed toward the group of Marwich boys that included Parker Marks. She stopped by the boys and started to talk. A second later she took Parker Marks's hand and led him out to the dance floor.

"I think I see what's going to happen," Roy said.

Heavenly and Parker started to dance. Hardly a minute passed before Samara crossed the floor and passed near them. Heavenly quickly reached out and grabbed Samara's hand. Samara, of course, pretended to be taken by surprise.

"She'll make a great actress," Roy said as Samara coyly pretended to be unsure if she wanted to dance.

"Oh, yes," I said with a chuckle. "She definitely will."

We shared a laugh as Samara and Parker Marks started to dance. Samara had a dreamy look on her face.

"She really looks like she's in heaven," Roy remarked.

Heaven, I thought and looked around for the person who I was sure had made this whole night possible. I found Heavenly coaxing yet another boy onto the dance floor. Just as Wes had predicted, once Heavenly got going, it wasn't hard to get everyone dancing.

Meanwhile Samara and Parker Marks kept going dance after dance. It looked like Samara was in love, and everyone else was having a great time.

Until I saw something that made my heart jump into my throat. Chance was dancing with Jessica! True, he was holding Tyler in his arms, but still.

"Is something wrong?" Roy asked.

"Uh, no." I shook my head and quickly looked away. I really didn't want to make a big deal about it. Instead, I picked up a big bottle of soda and started to pour it into cups. But my thoughts were a million miles away.

Why in the world would Chance dance with Jessica? I mean, talk about total opposites!

"Uh, Kit?" Roy said.

"Yes?"

"It really helps if you pour the soda *into* cups."

I looked down and saw that I was pouring soda

all over the refreshment table! I quickly set the bottle down.

"Sorry, Roy," I apologized and grabbed a bunch of paper towels.

"No problem," Roy said as he helped me mop up the spilled soda. "It's just that you weren't even close."

"It won't happen again," I said. "I promise."

Oddly, that was the last I saw of Chance and Jessica for the rest of the evening. Meanwhile, despite the weather outside, the gym actually started to get hot. Almost everyone was dancing. And I noticed that it wasn't just Soundview kids dancing with Soundview kids. A lot of them were dancing with Marwich kids, too.

"I can't believe Principal Jones's idea is actually working," Roy said as he used a paper towel to dab the sweat off his forehead.

"And I can't believe how much soda we're serving," I added.

"Guess you could say they're really dancing up a storm," Roy said.

"Drinking up a storm, too," I said, handing out cups of soda as fast as Roy could pour them.

"Too bad," Roy said. "I was kind of hoping we might get a chance to dance, too."

"Sorry, Roy," I said with a smile. "Maybe next time."

I hate to say it, but I didn't share in his disappointment.

Chapter

The he dance ended at 11 P.M., but it was after midnight when we finally finished cleaning up and got all of Wes's equipment back into the van. By then, just about everyone had left.

The storm had passed, and the rain and wind had pretty much ended. We gathered by the gym doors to make sure everyone was accounted for before we left.

"Where's Chance?" Robby asked, looking around.

"Right here." Chance came down the hall with Tyler curled up and asleep in his arms. Jessica was with them.

"What happened to you two?" Heavenly asked.

"Tyler started to get sleepy, so we decided to go someplace where it was quiet," Chance replied.

Just for an instant I thought I saw a knowing smile flash between him and Jessica. But then it was gone, and I began to wonder if I was just imagining things.

"Well, we're all here, so we'd better get going," Wes said.

We went outside. By now the van was the only car left in the school parking lot. We all climbed in. Wes said he'd give Jessica and Roy a ride home.

Inside the van, Samara leaned her head back at the roof. "Wow, that was the most perfect night."

"Things go well between you and Mr. Teen Model?" I asked.

"No comment," Samara said with a big smile.

"I still think it's amazing that the gym was the only place in the entire town that had electricity," Wes said as he turned out of the school parking lot. "I mean, it looks like the rest of the town is still dark."

I glanced over at Heavenly, who'd just reached for her left ear.

Twisting around in my seat, I looked back at the gym. It had almost disappeared behind the dark line of trees, but I thought I saw all the lights suddenly go out.

A split second later the school vanished in the dark.

Once again I wondered if I'd imagined it all.

The streets of Soundview Manor were still dark

and littered with leaves and tree branches. We stopped in front of Roy's house. In the windows we could see some candles flickering.

"This was really great," Roy said. "Thanks for helping me out, Kit."

"No problem, Roy," I said.

"Can I call you tomorrow?" he asked.

"Sure," I said.

Roy got out and went up the walk to his house.

"I don't see why he bothers to ask if he can call," Chance said with a chuckle. "You know he's going to call anyway."

"Yes, I know," I said wearily.

The next stop was Jessica's house. I guess I should say, Jessica's *mansion*, since that's really what it was. Strangely, the lights in her house were glowing brightly.

"I don't get it," Chance said. "How come your lights are on?"

"My dad had a generator system put it," Jessica explained.

"Wow," said Wes. "That must be some generator if it can light up the whole house."

"I guess," Jessica said. "I don't know much about it. But thanks for the ride."

"Any time," said Wes.

Jessica turned back to Chance and me. She flashed a big smile. "See ya."

"Right." Chance and I waved back.

Wes started to drive back down the driveway.

Heavenly was still staring back at the brightly lit mansion. "I thought you said her father had a pizza place."

"No, he owns a pizza company," Robby said. "Have you ever heard of Huffy's Pizza?"

"That man who's on TV all the time?" Samara said.

"You got it," said Robby.

Heavenly turned to Chance. "Isn't pizza your favorite food?"

"It is now," Samara said with a laugh.

"What do you mean?" I asked.

"Oh, nothing," she said.

Our house was the next stop. Through the kitchen window we could see the candles from the Chandler Self-Dousing Water Candle still flickering.

Wes thanked us all for helping him. And especially Heavenly.

Finally we all trudged into the house.

"Wow, what a night," Robby said with a yawn as we gathered around the candles on the kitchen table. Heavenly held the sleeping Tyler in her arms.

The puppy yipped and barked happily. Samara opened the crate and took him out. He licked her face.

"Ooh," she cooed, "look at the stormy little puppy."

"Hey," I said, "that's a great name!"

"Stormy?" Heavenly said.

"I like it," said Robby.

"So do I," said Samara. She held the puppy up and spoke to him. "From now on we're going to call you Stormy."

"So, did everyone have a good time?" Heavenly asked.

"Oh, yes!" Samara said dreamily. "The best!"

Chance nodded silently. I thought his eyes darted in my direction.

"I'm going to be a DJ like Wes when I grow up," Robby said. "That was cool."

"Maybe I'll be a professional dancer when I grow up," Heavenly said with a smile.

"I thought you were grown up," Robby said.

Heavenly smiled. "Maybe I'll never grow up. But right now I'm a professional nanny, and I have to put this little one to bed."

Heavenly carried Tyler out of the kitchen. Chance reached for the radio. "Maybe they'll know when the electricity's going back on."

"If the electricity's not on, how can you turn on the radio?" Samara asked as she played with the puppy.

"This one's got backup batteries," Chance answered. He turned the dial until he found the all-news station.

An announcer was saying that the entire area was blacked out, and it might be days before everyone got their electricity back.

It was late and we were all so tired that I don't

think any of us realized immediately what that meant. Suddenly Robby, Chance, and I all sat up and stared at each other.

"Wait a minute!" Robby cried.

"How is it possible?" said Chance.

"You tell me," I said.

"What?" asked Samara, as if she was suddenly shaken out of her dream.

"The radio just said there's no power anywhere around here," Chance said. "So how was there electricity in the gym tonight?"

"Who cares?" Samara said with a shrug and went back into dreamland.

"Here's another thing to wonder about," I said. "This afternoon when I left school, Jessica was in the middle of decorating the whole gym in brown. I wonder how it became gold and black and silver."

"Are you serious?" Chance asked.

"If you don't believe me, you can ask Jessica," I said.

"Okay, I will." Chance got up and pulled a piece of paper out of his pocket. Reading from it, he dialed a phone number. Suddenly I realized what that meant. Jessica had given him her phone number!

Chance waited while the phone rang, and then started to talk. "Hey, it's Chance."

"Oh, hi, I was hoping it was you," I heard Jessica say on the other end of the line. It was late and quiet enough to hear her through the phone.

She definitely sounded glad that he'd called.

Robby and I listened as Chance asked her about the decorations. Jessica confirmed what I'd said. When she'd left the gym that night to go have dinner before the dance, the decorations had been brown. She had no idea how they could have possibly changed between then and the start of the dance.

"Someone couldn't have come in after you and done it?" Chance asked.

"A hundred people couldn't have come in and done it that fast," we heard Jessica reply. *"I'm telling you, Chance, it was like magic."*

"Okay, thanks," Chance said.

"That's all you wanted to know?" On the phone Jessica sounded disappointed.

"Oh, uh . . ." Chance glanced at me. "See you around soon, okay?"

"Definitely," Jessica said.

Chance hung up the phone. "Should we go ask Heavenly?"

"Don't bother," I said as I watched a ladybug crawl across the kitchen table. "She'll never tell us. But it almost doesn't matter. I think Robby's right. I really think she is a Wiccan."

Robby and I turned to Chance and gave him a curious look.

"Do you believe us?" I asked.

In the flickering candlelight Chance rubbed his chin. "Wow, I don't know. On one hand, it's the kind of stuff I'd never believe. On the other, how else can you explain it?"

"What do we do now?" Robby asked, yawning again.

"Go to bed," I said. "But from now on, I think we have to watch her very, very carefully."

Chance nodded and smiled. "A Wiccan, huh? This could be incredibly cool!"

About the Author

TODD STRASSER has written many award-winning novels for young and teenage readers. Among his best-known books are those in the Help! I'm Trapped In . . . series. He has also written *Shark Bite Grizzly Attack, Buzzard's Feast,* and *Gator Prey* in the Against the Odds series, published by Minstrel Books. Todd speaks frequently at schools about the craft of writing and conducts writing workshops for young people. He and his wife, children, and Labrador retriever live in a suburb of New York. Todd and his family enjoy boating, hiking and mountain climbing.

You can learn more about Todd and the Here Comes Heavenly series at www.toddstrasser.com.